H.C. Gildfind lives in Melbourne and has published short stories, poetry, essays and book reviews in Australia and overseas. This collection was completed with the support of an Australia Council Grant and includes the award-winning novella 'Quarry'. Gildfind has researched interwar Australian literature and history, has been mentored by novelist Andrea Goldsmith, and is currently working on a novel.

Published by Margaret River Press in 2018

Margaret River Press
Web: www.margaretriverpress.com
email: info@margaretriverpress.com

Cover design: Susan Miller
Editor: Josephine Taylor
Typesetting: Susan Miller

Printed by McPherson's Printing

Cataloguing-in-Publication details are available
from the National Library of Australia
trove.nla.gov.au

ISBN: 9780648027577

THE WORRY FRONT

H.C. GILDFIND

MARGARET RIVER
·PRESS·

for Igor

CONTENTS

FERRYMAN

LAST NIGHT HE woke to squall thunder and the thud of something falling and he thought one thing—snow—and forced himself to sleep again so he wouldn't wake and worry about what fell and what might break in the night. And in the morning, it's here: fluffs of white on the car and roof and grass; hunks of blue-white ice blown and slapped onto the sides of the letterbox and the birch trunks and the wrecked stone wall; snow gone wet with rain and frozen again in the back and forth of the thrashing night; the trees strung with icicles, the lane turned into a back-breaking fairy-tale ice rink. Twice he's fallen, and twice he's gotten up and kept on going because if he doesn't walk he's gonna die. That's what the doctor said, that he's gotta walk his big fat gut off, he's gotta walk his plugs clean or he can just go and drop dead because if he won't look after himself then why the hell should anyone look after *him*? Eh? *Eh?*

He'd hated it at first. He was too slow and too heavy and everything hurt and he'd had enough of hurting, but it turns out it's his brain—not his body—that needs to be washed and washed in blood because every morning, warm and dumb with waking, he feels it all begin to shift in him. The words. The faces. Every morning he lies there numb and stuck in some sort of a forever déjà vu, watching everything that's happened re-member itself and uncurl itself and begin to circle itself around his head. Their words. Their faces. All of it starts circling, faster and faster, till his brain begs him out of bed because it learned quickly that if it pushes him into the cold and beats his feet on the ground his blood will pound in his ears and his breath will rasp out his mouth and his body will deafen itself from the inside out, from the outside in.

It's his first winter up here, the first time he's woken to a frozen storm and the first time he's walked on ice. He can't get the hang of it and he's shuffling sideways like a crab, shuffling slowly down the slipping lane. Too slow. The thoughts circle and circle, speeding up, spitting things out and sucking things in, like the morning radio and its drugs crashes rapes wars frauds tortures murders, a kid gone missing, and an old guy found dead—months dead—in his flat. And a baby, a baby shaken and shaken till its ribs got crushed and its neck clean broke in two. Though he's looking at his feet, all he can see is some stranger-man's hands around a baby's bird-chest and the baby's head flipping back, cartoonish, and how come the man's on trial when they said the mother might have done it too? How can that be? How can that be? And then he starts thinking of his girls and their tiny chests and necks and soft sweet heads and he thanks God he's reached the end of the lane and he thanks God someone came out in the night to grit the wide black road across the lane's end. He can walk properly now. He kicks up a stride and the salty gravel crunches rude and loud in the dead-dawn street and he scuffs his heels harder so it's louder and it carries him away, carries him away and over the hill and down to the steely water.

He turns right at the water's edge, his usual way. He swings his arms, punching the sky like an idiot but so what, so what. His blood races, chasing itself, washing him from the inside out, from the outside in. He swings and strides and stares across the cobalt water stretching from his feet to the far mountains glowing under the moonlit, dawn-lit caps of new snow. A turquoise streak cracks open the sky, widening and stretching, stealing the stars, igniting the day. Two ferries move back and forth, back and forth, luminous red against the silvery wet that pulls and puckers in their wakes, throwing back balls of white that fall from globes strung—row upon cold iron row—across the ferries' fat bellies, lighting the way from here to there, there to here. One of them draws close, speeding in to the launch, swinging its square bulk around—too fast, too fast—throwing up a foaming storm as it grinds to a stop. That's Kurt at the helm, having fun. Jim and Mick jump out with ropes and tie everything up and flip thumbs to Kurt and stand back as the steel drawbridge creaks down and the milk truck and the paper van and one lone car drive off and on their way. He marches by and waves to Jim and Mick and Jim and Mick wave back. As he goes he hears one say something and the other laugh something but he shrugs it off, he shrugs it off because they're the only guys he knows and they let him alone on his shifts and he likes them, he does, he does. Even if they don't like him, he likes them, and they're the only guys he knows.

He's walking hard, trying to pump warmth to his rubbery lips and prickling cheeks and frozen, gloved fingertips. He's finding his rhythm: the beat of his feet, the rasp of his breath, the arcs of his arms, the swing of his legs. On and on till his racing thoughts begin to slow to the tune of his movement, so he can see the faces, and hear the words, and attach the words to the faces. It's Millie and their girls: his daughters, her daughters. It's his sisters, Anna and Ellen, and his nieces, his nephews. It's his mum gone mute and his dad—understanding and not understanding, believing and not believing—caught between and spat out. It's his dad's heart—his own heart—pushing him through those flapping white doors. It's his dad waking up different, an old man. It's a three-line email, from his mother, last week. It's the radio news. And always, always, it's that little slut who started it all.

He walks faster. The oystercatchers stop for a second, pointing their stupid carroty beaks at him, checking him out and then turning back to the smooth black pebbles at their feet. Near them a crow hops back and forth, back and forth, stabbing at a plastic rubbish bag. The gulls wheel and cry, watching and waiting, watching and waiting, hanging out for whatever they can get and why not and who isn't? He walks on, sifting through those last few months, trying to lay them out, lay them bare. Trying to see what was right and what was wrong and what was real and what was not because it was those last few months—when he'd proven he'd done nothing; when that bitch admitted she'd lied—that really messed him up. And still, still, *still* he feels it, the sickening wave of horror as he'd realised it didn't matter that she lied because once they'd heard his name and that word—that filthy fucking word against his name—they'd never forget it.

He begins to run. His heart hammers in his ears and his feet slam on the ground and his knees jar under his gut, his disgusting fat gut. He focuses on the pain splinting up his shins and the ice-burn of his throat. He focuses on the silk water unspooling beside him and the night sky unthreading above him, and again he tells himself to forget it, forget it: he's here and not there, he's now and not then—but he'll never forget his girls. He'll never forget that they're little enough to forget him and what will Millie say when they ask where their daddy is? Stop it, stop it! You're north, not south. You're in the old world with a new name and a new job. You're a ferryman, a ferryman, just a guy getting people from here to there, from there to here, getting people across, keeping people safe, getting people home. But he can't stop anything, not while he's still struck by the paralysis that hit him as he watched the little slut wipe out his life—his *whole* life—with one single word. Still, he feels it, his moronic disbelief as he realised there was nothing he could do to stop her. Still, he sees them, the faces of all those people—so many fucking people—who suddenly appeared to help her, doing everything for her, everything, even afterwards, when she said she'd lied. How come no-one came to help *him*? He should have fucked her, fucked her dead. He should have fucked her dead.

The obelisk gleams ahead of him, its smooth marble bouncing back the hard white light from the clear sky and the snow, piled at its base. He reaches the memorial and seeks it out: that surname—the same one, repeated six times—in the middle of the list. For the hundredth time he presses his gloved palm to the chiselled and gilded letters, then bends down and digs out the wreath. He shakes the mushing snow from its fake and faded flowers and props it back against the stone and again he tells himself that he must bring something though he knows he'll forget because he always forgets. He turns and rests his back against the slab and looks down and across the water at the ferries moving back and forth, back and forth and tiny against the mountains they lace together. He lets their movement and the freezing column slow his thundering heart but nothing can calm the rage that roars through him every time the worst bit hits him. How it all got into his head. How he couldn't go near a kid without thinking all the filthy shit he knew they thought he was thinking. And they'd given him that teaching job 'cos they wanted men for their kids, for their fatherless kids, for kids like that goddamned little bitch. That's what they said, but now he knows what they didn't say, what they forgot to add: all cocks are suspect, all cocks are suspect, always, always.

His palms slap back onto the stone by his thighs, and again and again, harder and harder, till the wet freezes through his gloves and his skin stings sore, and he's slapping Millie and Anna and Ellen and his own damned mother. He's slapping that look off their faces as they watch him, hover over him, monitor him with their kids and his girls, for Chrissakes, his *own* little girls. *They're* the fucking perverts, pouring the filth from their heads into his so it's all he can think about and he might as well have fucked the bitch. Messed-up kid, they said, looking after her, looking after her. A kid? With those tits and that arse? With all that flirting, touching, teasing? He should have messed her up. He should have fucked her, fucked her like she begged him to. Should have fucked her dead.

He turns back and makes for home, wondering if the lane will thaw up there, on the hill; wondering if the icicles are dripping and wondering if anything broke in the night. He's lost his stride. His legs are weak and wobbly from jogging, his knees buckling under him, and he stops to rest again, watching the crow hop and tear at her rubbish bag; watching the oystercatchers search and search and the seagulls hover and cry, all of them out for what they can get and why not and who isn't? A gull lands near the crow and the crow rushes at it, cawing, her head low and her beak wide, her tail up, her neck feathers fluffed like a mane. She lunges and the gull trips and rises back into the air, floating up and down, while the crow returns to her bag, stabbing it and stabbing it and stabbing it with her granite beak. Then he's climbing over the rocks and down to the pebbles. The catchers scatter and the crow stops, staring as he comes closer. She hops slowly to one side, her head flicking and turning, watching him, watching him as he squats over the plastic bag and tears a hole in it for her.

A small blue fist. A small blue fist. A small blue fist clenched on itself; clenched on nothing. The ferryman watches two huge hands unglove themselves. They are massive, a man's hands. He watches them move the plastic away. He sees a baby's face, scrunched and bloated and blue. He sees a baby's face, brand new, brand new. The crow hops closer, curious, watching, wanting. The hands—pale and dry, disgusting—wave her back. The gulls lower, crying, watching, wanting. Again, the hands wave the birds back, then they slowly split the bag open along its length, unzipping it like a sleeping bag, from top to bottom, bottom to top. Gently, the bitten fingers wipe smears of food and coffee grounds from the tiny, shut-eyed face. Hold him. Gently, the thick, coarse fingers push wet paper and shredded plastic and shards of broken glass from the tiny, shut-eyed face. Hold him. Hold him. The hands disappear. The ferryman feels them cup his own elbows. He feels them cross his arms and push him backwards, onto his heels, so he's staring up into the snowed-out sky. Hold him. Something howls into the crisp, clear white. The giant icy paws cover the ferryman's ears, but still he hears it, something howling into the glare. It deafens him—the howling—it deafens him, from the inside out, from the outside in.

THE WORRY FRONT

ALL WEEK I have collected these small and delicate things. Ordinary things, but quite lovely really, once looked at closely. I spent Monday going about the house with a screwdriver, easing ball bearings from the runners of my sliding doors and windows. No mean feat, I tell you! I looked at them cupped in my pale hands, their black oil smudging up my dry old skin, and I saw such perfection, such fine crafting. How, I wondered, *did* they make them? Were they pressed out of metal? If so, how did they get them so perfectly round and all the same size? Or were they *com*pressed, somehow, from dust, from grains, from atoms? Then, in a flash, I saw the Big Bang, you know, that second of time—outside of time—when all of our worlds were wrought into the body of a small hard stone. A tiny ball of tension, the something before the everything, its boiling fronts forcing life and space and time into nothingness. True no-thingness. That's how Frank explained it. That we are forever travelling into the unmade, the unimaginable. That's how I understood him. Understanding. I looked at those ball bearings in my palm, and I realised that I did not know at all how they were made, that I did not know at all how anything is made, and that I never, ever would. Again, I was overwhelmed by the thought that has worried me all of my very long life. How I have not, and could not, know most of the wonders of this very big, very strange world. This is just a fact—but surely the overwhelming fact of everyone's life.

Now it's Friday, and I'm waiting in the thick-walled dungeon of a hospital. My appointment is at 4pm, but things are running a little behind time. I'm glad of this. It gives me a moment to focus my mind and explain to you—and myself—the hows and whys of what I'm about to do. So let me return to my recount of this rather strange week. Monday's collecting carried on into Tuesday, when I went through the drawers of every room, finding paper clips and safety pins, de-tacking thumbtacks, cutting off metal buttons, and sorting through my jewellery. Then, on Wednesday, I wandered into the shed: Frank's place. Such an unexpected comfort when, as if by instinct, I pulled on his dusty fleece, and then his old leather gloves—long worn to his hands' shape. I felt like I was wearing his skin. I sat down on the stool he once sat upon, I held the metal file he once held, and I began to shave the edges off the old tools he once treasured. Quite a pile of filings, I made. Really, I have left a wake of destruction on this journey. But who doesn't leave such wakes, no matter where they've been, no matter where they're going?

Yesterday morning I laid out my collection on the kitchen table. I stared at my trash—my treasure—and I braced myself for the step that is key to everything else succeeding: a day and a half of consumption. Goodness, I thought, that sounds biblical. Or tubercular. I laughed at that. Then suddenly, out of nowhere, the glittering wave of confidence that has pushed me through these months of waiting crested in me, poised—paused on my held breath—a shivering wall of salt water. I savoured that salt and tasted its true nature: not just confidence, but also a momentous grief. For a second I was confused. *Grief?* As I slowly recognised those unshed tears for what they were, I wondered, Why shouldn't grief and confidence coexist? Why shouldn't grief *be* confident? It, of all feelings, knows its object.

It's strange, you know, how I don't believe in God and yet I've prayed, prayed all my life. And yesterday, as I forced myself to exhale—slowly and fully, from the very depths of my belly—I prayed once again. Prayed that my plan was right and good. And guess what? A voice boomed back from within me! It commanded my tears to recede. They did. I looked again at my oddly beautiful buffet. The voice commanded me to eat it. I reminded myself of all I'd decided, all that I'd planned.

Reminded myself how, after long observing the slow movements of my body, I'd calculated that I must attempt to eat my metal bounty within a day and a half of this appointment. And now, as I wait in the bowels of the hospital, I hope and pray that a day and a half of ingestion and digestion has ensured not only that I've retained my loot inside me, but that it is spread evenly from my stomach to—well—my other end. Full to bursting, as the saying goes.

Anyhow, after that momentary hesitation—less a trembling than a mustering—a stronger resolve swept through me. I got Frank's old Italian coffee pot. I pressed the coffee into the metal filter, placed the filter over the water-filled base and firmly screwed on the top. I put the pot on the hotplate. I stood by and watched and waited, as I always do, and admired the fineness of its simple yet perfect design, as I always do, and I wondered vaguely— as I always do too—just where that pot has been and where it is still to go in its long life. Frank's friend bought it in Rome over sixty years ago. It was already second-hand back then and, solid as it is, I should expect it to move on through this world for years to come, jour- neying through time and space more than I could ever dream to. I waited and watched and wondered at the number of intimate conversations it must have witnessed in so very many kitchens. An oddly comforting idea but also, somehow, devastating: for a moment I was certain that the little pot had lived more than I! I veered from that feeling, that thought. Got busy fiddling with cups and cutlery until the pot began to spit and gasp. I took it off the hob and over to the table. I got Frank's big old enamel camping mug—another lasting, outlasting thing—and I filled it to the top. Stirred in a spoon of sugar. Then I put one teaspoon of de-tacked thumbtacks into my mouth and washed them down with a gulp of coffee. Nothing happened. If I baulked a little, it was because the coffee was too hot. I knew then—sweet relief!—that I could and would eat all that I had collected. My shivering wall of salt water—my confidence, my grief—had frozen into a pure and perfect conviction: I knew what I was doing; my plan, so far, was working. I sat there and stared at Frank's well-travelled pot and hoped that, though I may not have seen many wonders in this world, I might just turn out to be one of them.

So, on I went. I made my usual bowl of porridge with milk and a sprinkling of that fancy fibre mix Jenny gave me. (I'd thought that a rather pointed thing to give a woman entering her eighty-first year, but Jenny was just trying, as usual, to give me what she thinks I need. Dearest daughter. That's how she signed the card, 'From your dearest daughter'. Another assertion, another directive, another dig at Diana. Oh, I said a prayer when I saw that card. Prayed that something might save Jenny from herself, that something might save me from her, and that something—anything—might save docile, stupid Quentin and little Winnie too.) Anyhow, I sprinkled on Jenny's prescription, and then I sprinkled on my own: a tablespoon of ball bearings with a rather jaunty dash of metal filings. Careful not to chew, I ate the lot. It went down a treat. No problemo, as Angelo loves to say. No problemo, Gran! You know, I was actually beginning to enjoy myself. My breakfast didn't come back up, as I'd worried it would, and as I set about the rest of my to-do list, the food did not sit in me, hurting me, as I'd feared it should. Such relief—such a blissful rush of vertigo—as I watched my plan unfold so nicely.

Oh, this plan of mine! I've been plotting it from the very second when, in the shower nearly three months ago, I felt something strange under my skin: gnarled and hard, it spread through me like the aching old fingers of an unclenching fist. Oh yes, I knew what it was. No doubt this cancer has grown in my blood from the moment I was conceived. I've watched it consume my mother, my aunt, and my only sister. When I felt it, and recognised it, I waited for the Worry Front to storm my blood with terror—but strangely, nothing came. After a lifetime spent fearing things that, in the end, hardly ever happened, I did not feel afraid. Instead, I sensed something else entirely. At first the change was subtle: my brow and jaw relaxed (I had not realised, till then, they were furrowed and clenched). Then my neck and shoulders softened (I had not realised, till then, they were tied in knots). When my stomach muscles unlocked, I knew what was happening: the Worry Front was *finally on the move*. It suddenly rushed down through the rest of my body, and then? It disappeared—as if its wild forces had shot out of my toes and dissipated into the shower's clouding steam! Again, I pressed my hand into the lumpy newness I'd discovered growing within me. Never have I felt so calm. Never have I felt such a pure sense of power and purpose.

Now, let me backtrack a little to explain to you just what I mean by the Worry Front. I certainly knew my purpose in all those years I dedicated—heart, mind and body—to marching my lovely troop of little ones safely into adulthood. I knew my purpose, all right, but it did not fill me with a sense of power. Instead, at twenty-three, when my broken waters gushed away from me with Diana's birth, I felt something cold and alien rush into the void left by her hot little body: an icy flood of foreboding. That first night, in hospital, I clutched my baby close, and I told Frank how I felt. Poor Frank. I must have sounded mad! But he took my hand and listened as I told him how the familiar sea of my body had suddenly turned wild, assaulted by surge upon surge of feelings I'd never had before.

Dear Frank. He listened in his quiet, serious way. He did not doubt or mock me. Instead, after a moment, he cupped my face, then his daughter's, and said he understood. Said he'd felt a similar storm unleash inside of him when he first saw her. Said he felt like he was drowning in himself, like he could not breathe, like something huge was rushing in on him—invisible yet inescapable. And so, that night, when we named our first child Diana, Frank said we should also name the eerie new weather that came with her. The Worry Front.

That's what he called it, as if by naming it he could somehow contain it, control it, explain it. He reminded me of the many dark walls of cloud we'd watched rolling towards our home from across the sea. Those fronts brought terrible storms, yet all of them, he said, were merely caused by hot air hitting cold. I thought of the moment, just hours ago, when Diana's body left mine. I saw the inside world collide with the outside. I saw warmth and wetness hit cold dryness. I saw smallness and safety crash into a vast world of danger. Frank was right: that moment of collision created a darkness that moved straight into me. I could feel it, you know, as we huddled together in the hospital that first night. I could feel the darkness spreading through my mind—already raining terror down upon me. It will pass, Frank said. The weather always does.

But the Worry Front did not pass. As the days and weeks and years flew by, it became clear that nothing could tame the relentless storms it hurled through my body. How many sleepless nights did we spend lying in bed, gazing at each other, trying to push the front back with talk? How many times did Frank try to console me—and himself—by reciting aloud all the things that we knew to be true: anticipation is worse than realisation; it's pointless to fear things that you cannot control; dread is a terrible, terrible place in which to live.

But words weren't weapons enough. The Worry Front was powerful—more powerful than us. With the births of Ryan, Bradley, Rachel and—so very late and so utterly unexpected—Jenny, the front whipped up deeper and darker emotions. There were so many things that could hurt my children! But then, as they grew, it struck me cold to see them hurting each other, and Frank, and me, and—worst of all—the men and women drawn to their cool beauty and sparkling talk. For decades, my blood stormed away inside me. I'd ask Frank why the front didn't move on as he'd promised it would. He'd just shrug—helpless—until he finally confessed what he'd long suspected: the forces within it must be equal and opposite. The Worry Front just might be *stuck*. As practical as ever, he explained that stationary fronts were renowned for their relentless wild weather. I knew, then, that he had struck upon the truth of things. For the first time, I saw everything clearly: how, by constantly reaching for the future, my hopes and fears kept pulling that future back into the present, forcing the unknown to collide with the known, again and again. Bang, bang, bang! And, if the future was limitless? Well, so were my hopes and fears. No wonder my inner tumult never ceased!

This is what I mean when I refer to the Worry Front. It's the place—in my mind—where all these thoughts collide, creating the weather of my body. The place where I have lived my entire adult life. The place where I have always had a definite sense of purpose—to look after my family—but where I have always felt paralysed as I watched the front destroy present and future alike. So you can imagine my relief, three months ago, when I stood in the shower—my soapy hands tracing the hard ropey map of my fate—and felt the Worry Front rush away from me. After all these years I'd finally found the one thing that could rid me of its crashing forces: certainty. The present—with all its weight of the past—had finally outrun the future, neutering its dizzying possibilities with the promise of death. With the sweet relief of this certainty came an exhilarating pulse of power. I knew the path ahead. I knew that I would walk it. I knew, too, that I could—that I *must*—choose how.

So that night, I began to scheme. I awoke the next morning as excited and curious as a child on Christmas morning. I got dressed and trotted off to the doctor's to set my plan into motion. The dear young fellow looked at me steadily, frowning a little as I complained about some made-up old-lady thing: my womb, or its absence, was causing me all sorts of deep and painful problems. I told him of the troubles I'd had years ago, until he blushed at my real and invented intimacies. The poor man looked tired, and a little startled, and hurriedly did as I wished. A week or so later I received a letter from the hospital detailing this appointment. Luckily, I'd assumed correctly that I'd have to wait months to get this test, which has given me plenty of time to tie up my loose ends.

Visiting the lawyer and the bank was easy. But the vet? Well, that was a surprise.

Olivia was Frank's cat. He'd picked her up on the street one day, twenty years ago. He'd sold the shop and was out wandering the city looking for a job even though, by then, he was well over sixty. He said he'd felt a certain sympathy for her. They were both strays in a mean, anonymous place and he hoped karma might help him if he helped her. And, he said, *she* chose *me*. Apparently, she'd walked straight up to him and mewed, as coy and seductive as only a fluffy-white, green-eyed kitty can be. She leapt into his arms, tame and affectionate, and he took her straight home. Obviously, he'd stolen someone's cat. He knew it—he did—but neither he nor she cared, and from that moment onwards she climbed him like a tree, perching on his shoulder, claiming him as her own. They were a pair! If they didn't make each other so happy I'd have been jealous. Well—I must be honest now, for now is the time for honesty—I *was* jealous. Not just of her love for him, but of his love for her. When I watched them together, or when she'd sashay past me in the house—staring at me steadily with those clear and knowing eyes—I knew that she knew *she* answered something in Frank that I'd never even noticed. She was sensual, Olivia. *Sexy*, though it sounds wrong to say it. And they were all over each other, all the time. She lived in her body in just the same way I lived in the Worry Front. She lived in her body in just the same way, I realised—too late—that Frank lived in his.

Well, Frank up and died, didn't he? He was only seventy-five. But even in my shock I recognised Olivia's. In my stupor, I looked for her, fed and watered her, and made sure she was safe. After three weeks of keening—searching for him around the house and up and down the street—she finally seemed to understand that he was gone forever. One night, as I slept in the bed she'd never been allowed to sleep upon, she hopped onto my chest and nuzzled my chin. I—half asleep and not thinking—lifted the covers. In she crawled, as if she'd always done so, and nested in the curve of my stomach. I curled around her just as Frank used to curl around me. Of course I let her sleep there from then on. We had the same wound, didn't we? And thereafter, we stuck together. Not like she and Frank did, but in our own way. If she needed a scratch, I gave it. If I needed a hug, she let me. We kept a constant eye on each other, creating a new rhythm to heartsore days in a home that wasn't, after all, empty: there you are (Olivia appraising me from the window as I sat in the garden); there you are (me looking for her in the evening when it was time to watch TV); there you are, here we are, here I am. We weren't affectionate. Rather, ours was a practical, unsentimental and necessary cohabitation. We knew each other's needs. We agreed to provide. And so, with this new plan of mine, and her growing frailty, I saw my final obligation towards her as nothing other than that: practical, unsentimental, necessary.

I carried her to Dr Tilly's in my arms. Olivia would never lower herself to use a cage, and you can get away with anything at my age: who'd pick a fight with a little old woman and her little old cat? Olivia seemed content. She purred on my lap as we rode the bus. I stroked her—and let two small girls pet her—and watched as the streets I'd lived my whole life upon rolled slowly by, as familiar as Frank's coffee pot and mug. At Baker Street, the driver—a huge jolly fellow, apparently used to transporting ancient cats and ancient ladies—helped us off the bus. We walked the final two blocks to the clinic. When we got there, Dr Tilly met us in the reception area. She seemed to understand, if I did not, the import of what I was doing. She smiled at me, cooed over Olivia, and took me straight into the surgery.

A young nurse waited inside. Everything was laid out, ready, on a stainless steel table. Olivia, deeply senile, but as confident as ever of other creatures' adoration—in this regard always more dog than cat—had no idea what was happening. All she did was flick and then lower her ears and query me with her enormous eyes when the nurse started up the clippers. She wasn't afraid, it was just new to her, as this plan of mine is new to me. She batted at the clippers as if they were a toy, making us laugh. We let her. We pretended we were playing her game, and not God's. We chatted to her as the white fur was sheared from her foreleg. We fussed over her when she flinched as the catheter pierced her pale, newly exposed skin. And even then, somehow, she remained unfazed, still basking in our attention. She head-butted my chin, purring so loudly I'm sure her own deaf ears could hear her satisfaction. The vet picked up a syringe full of green fluid. And then, suddenly, Olivia lay very softly, very warmly, and very limply in my arms.

I started to cry. If those tears were a surprise to me, they weren't to Dr Tilly. She put her arms around me and said that Olivia was lucky to have had me, and that I'd done a merciful thing. I just nodded, signed a piece of paper, and let them waive the fee it cost for them to do what they had done, and were yet to do, with her body.

I walked home slowly, after that. It was a long walk for me, but I just could not face a bus full of people. Could not face retracing—alone—my last moments with Olivia. And still I cried. I wasn't sobbing: it was more like my tear ducts were broken and leaking. I walked and cried and as I neared my house—which, for the first time in my life, was truly empty—I understood my tears: Olivia was Frank's cat, and for so long as she lived so did my most intimate connection to him. The children unite us—of course they do—but that link is different: less like a single strand of silk than a tangle of sticky threads. Strange, how it took Olivia's death to make me truly comprehend Frank's. Before then, I simply hadn't believed he could be here—one second— and gone the next. He must have gone *some*where, surely? As I stepped into my silent house that afternoon, I finally knew the answer to that question: *No.* Frank was gone. He was nowhere. And he'd lied to me. He'd said it was impossible to imagine nothingness. But that day, I did better than imagine it: I *saw* it. Nothingness. True no-thingness. It looked just like life without him.

Putting Olivia to sleep was the most difficult thing I've done these past few months. Everything else—the doctor, the lawyer, the bank, and this week of collecting and consuming my metallic feast—was a breeze, in comparison. The only other exceptional thing I've done is turn eighty. I didn't want a party, but the children said it was a landmark that *must* be celebrated. That's my children, always ticking boxes that others assert the value of. For them, the principle of the thing always matters more than the thing itself.

And so, it began. Jenny stated that a party would be held at her place, and began issuing orders to the others. Bradley said he wanted to host it in his new 'bachelor pad' in town, where we could celebrate my birthday and his divorce from 'that bitch' Sharon. Ryan and his new baby-faced wife, Elise, were on a cruise and sent an email declaring they'd book a house on the coast, so we could have a whole weekend away together, which even I could see was absurd. In the end, Diana simply went ahead, in her viciously pragmatic way, and booked a set-menu dinner at her city restaurant: very expensive, very formal, and perfect for rubbing her siblings' faces in it. (It is still a mystery to me where her wealth—and meanness—comes from.)

After many tearful phone calls from Jenny, the big day finally arrived. She and Quentin appeared at the door. Stony-faced, with dry kisses, they wrapped me up in a blanket and plonked me in the back of their old station wagon. Submerged in dog hair, toys and dried-in food, Winnie cast me a long-suffering look from her hot-pink booster seat. Though she was dressed in a purple fleece jumpsuit, and wore knee-high yellow gum-boots—whose toes were moulded into the beaky faces of ducks—and though she is barely four, she emanat-ed the solemn weariness of an old woman. This we had in common. As the car lumbered down the road and nosed towards the city, Winnie clutched my hand and kept looking from me to her silent parents, as if we could somehow decipher, without words, the mystery of their infinite inexplicable tension. Poor Winnie: old enough to sense something is wrong, but too young to know what or why. I held her hand tightly, but I could not meet her bewildered gaze. Instead, I looked outside. I can't bear to think of what she has seen—and will see—unfold between those parents of hers.

At the restaurant, Diana sat at the head of a bur-nished wooden table. Her staff looked stricken. When she wasn't surveilling them, she stared over her stylish glasses at Bradley. He was already drunk and blustering about Sharon, even though Angelo was sitting right next to him. Soon enough, Angelo shoved his phone into his pocket, stood up and stormed outside. Propelled by a warning glare from Diana, Bradley followed. I'm sure I saw a smirk flicker across her face as she watched him go. Did she, I suddenly wondered, host us at the least fami-ly-friendly of her restaurants to treat us, or to express her contempt for 'breeders'? (That word—her word—still cuts me to the quick.) Father and son soon returned, grinning shamelessly, Angelo making no attempt to hide the money he'd just been given. I saw then how generously Bradley rewarded behaviour like his own. And I saw how Frank and I must have rewarded such behaviour too. How else did Bradley grow to be so aggressive, so entitled, so self-sorry? Eventually Ryan and Elise flew in, an hour late and as unapologetic as ever. They dumped poor cross-eyed, moon-faced Jack onto my lap, ordered Charlotte to sit beside me, and went to fawn over Diana. That left Bradley ranting at nobody, Angelo and Charlotte absorbed in their phones, and Jenny and Quentin stranded with me, Jack and Winnie. As usual, no-one mentioned Rachel or the fact that, once again, she hadn't turned up.

It was, in all, as strained a meal as ever—an exhausting navigation around sensitivities and triggers that I just cannot keep track of anymore. For hours we sat there, chatting and eating, each playing our part in a painful pantomime of what I'd always thought would be mine: the big family; the manifestation and evolution of love in all its forms, through all our lives' stages. I was so naïve! I knew nothing about the love and un-liking of families.

Finally, a huge white cake appeared—more wedding cake than birthday cake—borne forth by a singing waiter. It had eight candles, as if I were a child again. I asked Charlotte to blow them out. That was the first and last time she looked up all night. I gazed into her clear blue eyes, and I wondered how she—with her acne and her braces and her awkward, lanky body—was coping with her father's remarriage to such a young and glamorous woman. Charlotte answered me with one of her rare sad smiles, and disappeared back into her screen. Whilst I'll never forget that sweet gift, I hardly noticed the other presents that were then passed my way. I was too busy battling against the sadness that was filling me up as I admitted to myself that perhaps, after all, my children had not grown into very nice people. How, I wondered, had Frank and I failed to teach them the most important thing of all: how to love?

When I was a girl, all I wanted was to fall in love! That sounds so pathetic now, even to my old-fashioned ears. And yet, my good luck was that I *did* fall in love, and with a decent man. Somehow, Frank and I understood that love cannot be planned for, and so we worked hard to make sure our babies had choices. We wanted them to have some control over their lives. We wanted them to be educated, to get decent jobs—some financial security—so they could enjoy all that the world might offer them. At my eightieth, as I watched my children spar with each other, I saw how well we'd taught them. We gave them choices, and they have forever been anxious over those choices. We valued control, and now they try to control everything—and everyone—around them. We wanted the world to be theirs, and now they feel entitled to the world, to *all* of it. As I sat there— as relaxed as anyone can be in a minefield—I saw how sophisticated Frank and I had made them. Too sophisticated to love, or be loved. To be kind, or to accept kindness. To just be together, accepting themselves and each other, just as they are. For the first time, I truly understood what Frank and I had done. We bred our children to compete, and if life is a competition, then everything and everyone must always seem a threat.

I sat between silent Charlotte and sulking Jenny, pondering all of this. Awkwardly—for darling Jack slept on my lap—I pushed my cake around my plate and tried to ignore the disappointment swelling through me. But I couldn't, just as I couldn't ignore the sniping of my children. So I faced that disappointment head-on. This is what I saw. *I* chose to have my babies, they did not choose to be had. They did not choose me, or Frank, or each other. Why *should* they like each other? Why *should* they love each other? And who was I to burden them with such desires and expectations? On the night of my eightieth, I realised that it was I, and not they, who was the source of my disappointment. If I truly cared for them, rather than myself, the only question that mattered was why, even with the choices they *do* make, are my children still so unhappy?

I put down my spoon and hugged Jack ever closer. I looked around the table. I studied each of my children's beautiful faces for the very last time. I looked, and again—with a shudder—I made myself see what I saw.

The Worry Front.

That's what my children's brittle smiles struggled to contain that night: the relentless wild weather whipped up by nothing less than the Worry Front. Had the front been passed on from us to them like a genetic disease?

Was it the same front? Or did each of them form a storm system of their own, born from their own ways of thinking and being in the world? Perhaps. But who taught them how to think? Who taught them how to be? I did. And Frank did.

Yes, Frank and I loved each other deeply, but—first and foremost—we were fearful people. And that's what we taught our children from the second they entered the world. Not to love first. But to fear first. And how can one love, if one is always afraid?

I made myself look at each of my grandchildren. Made myself see what I saw. Oh yes, the Worry Front had them too. Already, the turgid black clouds of their parents' anxieties were creasing their young faces with tension. Already, they'd been taught to fear.

I turned away then. I sank my face into the sweet fuzz of curls that crowned Jack's silly-shaped head, and I waited for the night to end. And eventually it did, as all things do.

So, that was my eightieth: an enforced celebration of a very long life that I was only just beginning to understand. Apart from that dinner, killing Olivia, and harvesting and eating scraps of metal, I have carried on a completely normal life these past few months. I have filled my time with my usual activities—cleaning, cooking, shopping, gardening, reading—whilst patiently counting down the days to this very important week and these final stages of my plan.

Which brings me back to yesterday, when I dined

as I've never dined before. Crackers with cream cheese and paper clips. Endless cups of tea and coffee, sweetened with sugar and ball bearings. A tumbler of red wine with a teaspoon of tiny, pretty cogs from a dozen knick-knacks. Mashed potatoes with more ball bearings and, for dessert, ice-cream mixed with all that was left over. Though I was far too full, I did not feel sick as I sat down to watch TV. No, there was only that sharp stab of pain when—automatically—I called for Olivia, then remembered she would not be sauntering in to sit with me.

I turned on the TV and looked at the coffee table: staring back at me was my last task for the day. Five pieces of paper and five envelopes. Five letters to write, to post on the way to this appointment today: like the ingestion of my collection, this task was also a matter of careful timing. I turned the TV low, picked up a pen, and focused on the blank pages. Nothing happened. This was the first part of my plan that, clearly, I had not really thought through. I had nothing to say. Or too much to say. Or nothing that I should say, or could say. What *can* a mother say to children who are so deeply wounded and wounding? I love them so very much— but far too often, I do not like them at all.

So I left those pages blank, last night. I put them in their envelopes, addressed them, and posted that blankness to each of them on my way here today. They're clever, my children. I'm sure they'll work out just what it was I wanted to say.

The nurse, a young man, is calling my name. I ease myself up to standing. Though every part of me hurts, I love this dear old body of mine: it has, after all, given me a home to live in all of these years. The nurse smiles. He threads my hand through his elbow and we walk down the gleaming white corridor like an old married couple. He takes me into a tiny room. He sits me down and asks me reams of questions. I answer with lies: No, no, no. I have never been a welder. I do not have a pacemaker. I do not have any prosthetics. (Oh, but I do—a hip, and a knee or two.) No, I'm not wearing any jewellery. (At least this is true, for my jewels are inside me now, swallowed down with a froth of hot chocolate.) On he goes, looking at my face, checking to see that I—such an old, old lady—can hear and understand him.

And this is another part of my plan that I failed to think through. I forgot that I would sit across from someone—a real person, not imagined—and I would lie to them. Momentarily speechless, I stare into the boy's lovely brown eyes: in all my life I never planned for the kindness of strangers, just as I never planned for the unkindness of my children. The nurse's skin is dark, and his hair is as thick and black and shiny as oil. How old is he? Twenty? Thirty? *I did not plan for this.* How could I forget that, inevitably, I would do to others what I have chosen to do to myself?

That shivering wall of salt water—my confidence, my grief—crests in me. Poised. Paused on our locked gaze. I inhale. When I exhale, a voice—the God I pray to?—booms back from deep within me, commanding my tears to recede. They obey. The voice commands me to fulfil my plan. I must. I will.

The nurse asks me if I am okay. I smile. He asks me if I am ready. I nod. He helps me get undressed: through some strange magic, he protects my modesty whilst changing me into little more than a blue paper smock. Then he walks me across a corridor and into a dark room whose walls are starred with hundreds of tiny lights. A woman sits at a sloped, sparkling table: she could be a pilot, sitting in the cockpit of a plane. She smiles and talks me through everything we are about to do. She nods at the nurse, who takes me into a room next door. Everything in here is white, including the machine. It looks space-age, like something that might orbit the earth. Well, today it will orbit me. The nurse helps me onto the bed, squeezes my hand, and then he is gone.

I am alone. It is quiet. After a moment, my bed slides into the machine's hollow centre. My heart flutters crazily for a second. I realise my eyes are screwed shut. I open them. The top of the tunnel is just inches above my face, as if I'm already in my coffin. I giggle, then, as all of my plan's grandiosity hits me. You vain, silly old woman! This won't transform you into a wonder of the world. More like a blunder! Less a Big Bang, than a Big Splat!

A voice comes through the machine: You okay, sweetheart?

Is *this* the God I pray to? No. It's just the radiographer checking I haven't started to panic.

Honey, you okay?

I tell her I'm doing just fine.

As the machine begins to whirr and click, alien feelings spark to life inside me. Not fear. Not anxiety. But curiosity, excitement. Strange, how these new feelings don't, after all, feel so very different to the old.

The machine jackhammers fully to life. It's so loud. I sense its huge and heavy rings circling me. Throughout my chest and stomach and below—where my womb once was—I feel a rush of prickling. Pleasure and pain, all at once. A deep unscratchable itch.

As the machine gets louder, the prickling unifies into a whole-body tugging. Perhaps my skeleton will leap out of me in one piece! Imagine it! Perhaps I didn't need to eat my metallic buffet. Perhaps the iron in my blood was enough, all along, to draw me out of myself and launch me into this world that I never really understood, and never really got to see.

The forces upon and within me get stronger, but I just close my eyes and relax into my body's new weather. I wonder what will happen to my belly full of gunshot. I wonder what will happen to my memories of Frank and the children and Olivia. I wonder, most of all, what will happen to my body, and to whatever else it is that makes me who I am.

When the pain hits, it's a pain like no other. But I do not flinch. Instead, I turn my mind to it. I seek it. I find it. I let it find me. Quickly I begin to sink under the very same waves of agony that are bearing my body away from me. Such a curious feeling! To move inwards and outwards, all at once. To end and begin, all at once. To wonder, instead of worry.

Then, all is black and still and silent. And I see it. That moment before the Big Bang, when the universe was wrought into the body of a small hard stone. A tiny dot of tension. The nothing before the something, before the everything.

And though I don't believe in God, I pray. I pray for my life.

GENTLY, GENTLY

GENTLY, YOU PLACE them on the back seat. Soft rustles from inside. Dry scrape of claw. Papery flutter of feather. Low clucks, but not many. They're quiet. They're frightened, trying to find their feet in the slipping dark. This morning you stabbed air holes into the box's sides with a kitchen knife. Now you squint through the gouges, trying to see if they can see you. A reptilian yellow eye stares back. Another scuffle. The lizard of look flashes away.

You both move to the front of the car. He walks to the driver's side. You follow. You put your hand out for the keys. 'No need,' he says, opening the door. He is just trying to help. Head averted, you nudge him away. Carefully, you drive down the farm's gravel drive. You sense his hurt. You ignore it. You turn onto the dirt road. You

43

concentrate on its rutted, pot-holed surface and try to ignore the distress pulsing from the back seat. You can't.

You're back on the highway. He's talking about something. You stare at the broken white lines on the strip of black, tick tick ticking past. A woman in an old station wagon overtakes you on the right. In her back seat, a little boy sits next to a grey plastic baby carriage. He is smiling and watching the pale flashing stars of his tiny hands in the rear-view mirror. Just a broken white line, tick tick ticking between you. You watch it unfold.

A mere flick of the wrist.

Your car nicks theirs.

They ricochet across the highway, slamming into a ton of roadside gum.

The rough embrace of steel.

But your mind's eye is not interested in this image: a clichéd scene from a bad movie. Instead, it is watching three escapee chickens belt themselves against your own car's windows, a blizzard of feathers as they bat around and around and around a car that is spinning out to nowhere.

Your stagger of laughter.

He smiles, thinking you are laughing at something he's said.

Ø

You get home at lunchtime. Together, you stand in your small backyard. The box sits between you on the grass. You have spent the past week knocking together a coop from old wire, wooden crates and rough-sawn branches. It's not beautiful, but it's sturdy. They have everything they need: roosts, nesting boxes, and a wire floor to repel the nocturnal prowls of cat and fox. During the day they'll roam the yard.

Again, you ask him if he's sure that the six-foot fence is high enough.

Again, he tells you everything will be fine. 'Trust me,' he says. He squats down and lifts the cardboard flaps.

Inside, your three birds are plumped up in a fluff of defence. Their heads twitch at the sudden light.

'Out you get,' he says. He peers in at them, his elbows resting on his bent knees. His sleeves are rolled up over his firm, dark forearms—the ropes of vein and sinew that make him up.

He starts making wet kissy noises.

You shake your head.

'What?' He squints up at you and the midday sun.

He tries to make clicking sounds, as you do with the dog. He sounds like he is choking on his tongue.

'Stop that,' you say. 'It's disgusting.'

The birds just sit there, a little less round, a little more curious, their heads craning left and right as they calculate the stupidities of their new situation.

You step forwards and kick the box onto its side.

'Hey!' He rocks back onto his heels and stands as the birds somersault and slide onto the grass, shrieking. Quickly, they right themselves and shake dignity back into their plumage. They begin to walk in circles, stopping now and again to stretch out their wings and legs: chicken-style yoga. Then they set to work exploring the yard. They scuff up the grass and the soil, kick about the gravel, peck at the dirt. Occasionally they fly at the air, looking demented, and you wonder if they've been brain-damaged somehow by the drive. You realise they are catching bugs.

After a while, feeling encouraged, you release the dog into the yard. She leaps out from the laundry, where she's been crying this whole time, and bounds after the chickens. Confused about which one to chase, she inadequately chases them all. The birds squawk and jump, but they seem more affronted than afraid, as if wondering what this foolish creature is doing in *their* yard.

Soon enough, the dog flops into a pile of geriatric exhaustion at your feet. She cries under her breath, her grey-flecked chocolate snout sniffing the air as her eyes flick between each of the alien creatures. One of them struts up and scratches dirt across her splayed paws. The dog looks up at you with dark mournful eyes.

'So,' he asks, hoping for a reprieve, 'back to work?'

You nod.

Though neither of you want to leave your new pets, there are things that need to be finished.

Ø

Last night, you painted the ceiling, the skirting and the windows. The hard stuff is done. All you need to do now is fill in the blanks of the walls. You've chosen the colour already. A deep yolky yellow. A simple gesture towards health.

He's still annoyed at your insistence that this one room be painted. 'Why?' he keeps asking. 'This is stupid. It'll just make the rest of the house look shitter.'

'Shitter?' you repeat, as you cover each of your brushes in plastic wrap. It's time to check the chickens.

'Yes,' he says, 'shitter.' He comes up to you and grabs your backside. 'Now *that's* a shitter,' he says, giving it a rough squeeze. 'Mmmm-mmm.'

'Get lost!' You pull back, turning your smile away from him.

You haven't justified your need to paint the room beyond, Just because, Just because. Perhaps, after all, there'll be no need to explain anything.

You both go outside to check if the chickens are in the coop. It is dusk and every colour glows with defiant intensity. The camellias are redder than red, the lavender more purple than purple, and the lemons are surreal luminous lamps, set deep into satins of green. For a second, the colours stop you both at the door, disoriented. Then you remember the coop.

It is empty.

Your stomach clenches.

Standing still, you both look around the quiet garden.

At first, nothing.

Then, sweet relief: you spot one of the birds wedged into a low fork of an apple tree. Her head is wobbling.

She is half asleep, half awake.

'Hello girl!' he yells, so that she rocks up to standing, ready to flap away.

'*Stop* it,' you whisper. You point across the yard. 'Look.'

A second bird is roosting on the dowel of an old deckchair.

You search on, those first seconds of relief bowling away as you realise what has happened. You feel sick. 'Idiots,' you say. '*Idiots.*'

In a daze, you shush the two surviving birds into the shadowed coop. Somehow, they know what to do. With some sleepy clucks and half-hearted bullying they settle next to each other on the leaf-stripped branch that you have wired up for them.

He is standing at the back door, watching.

You can't meet his eye.

You push him aside as you try to go back into the house.

'Watch it,' he says, holding your arms, barring your way. 'We'll find her.'

And suddenly, you're going for him. Hitting his chest. His gut. His face. '*Why* do I listen to you? *Why* do I listen to you?'

'Don't!' He shoves you back clumsily. 'Stop it!'

There's a crack in his voice. You wonder if it's for you or the lost bird.

You can't get past him.

You return to the coop. The two chickens are asleep

now, their heads folded under their wings, their bodies snuggled close together for warmth. 'It's my fault,' you say. At the sound of your voice, one of the birds pulls her head out and looks at you, clucking a little, as if telling you that she's not interested and please be quiet because can't you see that she's trying to get some shut-eye?

'It's *my* fault,' he says, behind you. He tries to pull you into a hug.

You shrug him off.

For hours, armed with a torch, you wander the streets alone, looking for her.

Ø

You give up at midnight. It's cold and wet and you've returned with nothing other than a hundred gut-wrenching images of what might have happened to her. Nothing but fury at your own stupidity and rage against a world that will laugh at you for caring. It's just a chicken, just a chicken, you tell yourself. It's just a fifteen-dollar bloody chicken. But even as you try to convince yourself that it is just an it, you know that it is a she, and she has a name and, after all, he is just a man and you are just a woman and nothing, *nothing*, is ever just anything.

Your feet are burning. You wonder, vaguely, if all this upset and all this walking will resolve that other problem for you. You remember reading of a woman who walked twelve hours a day and took flu tablets till she was free of hers. You couldn't understand, back then, how all the while that she walked and doped herself stupid on quinine, she spent her nights knitting tiny sets of clothes. Now, you think you get it. It was just in case, just in case. It was just in case nothing turned out to be something after all.

When you return home, you go straight through to the backyard to see if some strange animal instinct has brought her home. She's not there.

Back in the house, you find him in the half-painted room. He is sitting on the floor, propped against the wall, facing the window. He is drunk and still drinking, listening to the radio and humming along to some rockified song about Jesus. The dog lies on the floor next to him, her head heavy on his lap.

'Close the door, 'scold,' he says.

You pull the glass door shut behind you, and edge across the paint-spattered sheeting to the window.

'Thanks for your help,' you say, gesturing at the unfinished walls. 'Too busy doing nothing?'

He doesn't look up. He just keeps patting the dog, his long, slow strokes pulling up the dark brown lids of the animal's soft half-closed eyes. The dog grumbles in her sleep: half growl, half purr.

'Why aren't you painting?'

Gently, he moves the dog's head off his lap and onto the floor.

He stands up, one hand pressed hard against the plaster-patched wall. He spends a moment flicking dog hair off his jeans as if it is for this reason, and not his drunkenness, that he needs to steady himself. Finally, he looks at you. 'Because,' he says, 'I couldn't be *fucked*.'

He's looking for a fight, and so are you.

He lurches towards you. Jabs a finger into your shoulder.

If he knew, you think, he wouldn't do that. You correct yourself. You don't know what he'd do, if he knew.

You thump his shoulder with the palm of your hand. Again, you ask him why he hasn't finished the room. Again, you thump him, right where he once broke his collarbone.

He stumbles backwards. In slow motion, he finds his feet.

You have never seen him so drunk. He looks like he's about to throw up, and when he leans in close you can smell the sour hours he's been sitting in here, alone.

'Everything,' he says, 'isn't always, *always* my fault.'

He swings away from you, but turns too sharply.

He trips.

His hand flies out to steady him.

For a second, you can see exactly what is about to happen. Some quick part of you grabs the dog's collar and jerks her back from the door.

The crash of glass.

The whine and snap of wood.

Barking.

His voice. High-pitched with drink and fear. Swearing. 'Fucking idiot,' he's saying. '*Fucking* idiot.'

He's tripping away down the hall.

You stand right where you are, staring at the shattered door. Knife-edged stretches of glass lean out from the wooden frame, precarious. There's glass on the carpet. There's blood on the glass. There's blood on the door. Blood on the floor.

Barking, barking. The dog is straining away from you, yearning to help.

Your body continues to take control.

Your free hand is opening the window. You are squatting down and putting your arms under the frantic dog's belly. You are heaving her up. She stops barking. Her legs go limp. Clumsily, you lift her out the window and then drop her gently into the overgrown dark of the garden. She begins to bark again. You stare at your bare feet, watch them climb you out of the window too. You wander to the coop and look in on the sleeping birds. They're fine and you could stare at them for hours but the barking dog stops you. You think of the neighbours. You lock her in the laundry. You scatter dry dog food on the concrete floor to distract her. You hear the tap running in the bathroom. You hear mumbling. You realise he's crying. Suddenly you're running down the hall.

His hand is under the gushing tap. He is looking at the wall. He is shaking all over. He does not look at you. He simply holds his hand out towards you, his face turned away.

His hand and wrist are covered in blood: pink where it mixes with the water; red where it comes, and keeps coming, fresh from his wounds.

There are swerves of blood on the floor.

There's a smudge of red on the light switch.

'It's okay,' you say. 'It's okay.' Gently, you take his hand in yours. Where one of his knuckles used to be, it now looks as hard and as white as the ball of an eye.

'Is it bad?' he asks.

You shush him. Around the edges of the wound you can see the depth of his skin, a miniature cliff face, weeping. You tell him to bend his finger. He winces, but he bends it. Your fingers are warm and slippery in his clutch. You turn his hand over to see. A deep gash runs the length of his palm. It severs his heart and life and head lines. You smile at the poetry of it. You recoil. It's not an idea, you tell yourself. *He* is not an idea. He's hurt.

'How is it?' His voice is slow, thick from the drink and the shock. 'What've I done?'

'You'll be okay.' You reach for a facecloth and, with one hand (for you cannot let go of his), you fold it into a narrow strip. You wrap it tightly around his finger. You get another towel and bunch it into his cut palm. You firm his unhurt fingers around the bulge of fabric and drape the rest of the towel over everything. Blood immediately begins to blotch through the material, spreading, spreading. You place his hand up on his shoulder so he cannot see it. 'It's okay,' you say. 'It's okay, but you have to go to hospital.'

He nods.

'I can't leave the dog here, with the glass. She'll keep

barking if I keep her locked out.'

Again, he nods stupidly.

'I'll call you a taxi.'

'Idiot,' he mutters. 'Useless fucking idiot.'

You sit him on a chair by the front door and make the phone call and, as you do, all the 'what ifs' surge through you. You see the dog's paws pressing into the glass, the big shards slicing and the tiny splinters pressing right up and forever into the intricate webs of skin between her rough paw pads. What if, what if. You see him falling into the glass again, the weight of his body pushing his wrist right through, this time, so that the cut on his palm reaches up the inside of his arm, tearing his wrist open. What if, what if. Again you see him fall into the door, this time face first, skull first. See the two of you scuffling, so it's your arm, your face, your skull. And you are horrified. Horrified that it's not horror that you feel upon these thoughts, but shame. Not shame at what you've become, but shame at the knowledge that such wounds need explaining, that such wounds are windows through which people can peer in at the lives that you lead.

You put his phone in his pocket with his wallet and keys. 'You could have killed yourself,' you say. 'You could have hurt the dog. You could have hurt *me*.'

He looks like he is about to faint.

'Do you understand?'

Nothing.

Ø

You put slippers on and return to the half-painted room with a dustpan and vacuum cleaner. You squat down and begin to pick up the biggest bits of glass. No matter how careful you are, you keep cutting the tips of your fingers, your blood mixing with his.

Once the largest pieces are removed, you brush up the rubble and the splinters. You're sure a cloud of glass-dust covers your skin. That you're breathing it in. That it's settling into the soft, wet sponges of your lungs and the wet-lidded edges of your eyes.

Finally, you have vacuumed all that you can: the plastic sheeting and the carpet underneath; the lino; even your slippers and jeans and the sleeves of your jumper.

With the floor cleared, you can no longer avoid the broken door. For a while you just stand there, staring at the web of cracks and the jagged shards leering out from the old frame.

You go to the laundry to get a roll of masking tape. The dog is fast asleep: her second dinner has knocked her out cold. You lean down and press your fingers against her freezing nose. Her eyes open. Sleepily, she begins to lick the blood off your hands. You pull back, remembering the splinters. You wrap one arm around and under the floppy warmth of her neck and lift her heavy head up a little, hugging her as she licks the salt off your chin.

You return to the shattered door. Slowly, you begin to ease the broken pieces back into the frame. You aren't sure if you're doing the right thing, but you don't even want to try lifting the daggers of glass up and out of the casing. You'll cut up your hands. You'll drop them on the tops of your feet. You'll trip on them as you carry them away and just where would you put them anyhow?

For hours, it seems, you keep on working, gently realigning the edges of the glass where they can be re-aligned, then covering up the cracks and filling in the gaps with tape.

When you are finished, the glass door has transformed into a sheet of cream-coloured blood-smeared paper. Your fingers are stained and stinging.

Again, you vacuum the plastic sheeting and the carpet and the lino, looking for anything that might have fallen as you worked. The more you vacuum, the more shards you find. Every time you turn one way, a sparkle in the corner of your eye turns you back again. All you can do is run the vacuum again and again over the same spot, knowing that if you replace the carpet, or lay a new rug, or even if you move houses, you will always be standing in one spot, searching out the splinters.

Ø

You go to bed, but when you can't sleep you get up and keep working on the room. Now, at four in the morning, you're finished. He still isn't home from the hospital.

You shower and change into your pyjamas.

As you walk back to the bedroom, you hear it.

A metallic scratch.

A dry scuffle.

A thud and a rustle.

You wander around the quiet house, trying to pick where the sound is coming from. It's not inside. You go out into the backyard. Nothing. You walk around the edges of your house. You walk out to the street. You scan your neighbours' dark gardens. You stand in the silence and the cold and the breath-held damp, waiting.

Nothing.

Then, again: a thud. You look towards the sound, and you see it. Something moves in the moon-shadows of your neighbour's roof.

This bird that can't fly is perched high up in a clutch of night, right where the second-storey roof meets the first. Below her, the corrugated iron slopes steeply to the eaves.

You watch her. Each time she slips, threatening to tumble to the gutters, she scuffles and flaps about, getting her grip. As you watch her, you realise that she keeps slipping because she keeps falling asleep.

'Silly girl,' you whisper, then fear overrides relief as you see that she's exhausted, and maybe she's hurt, and you have no idea how to help her.

The street and the bird suddenly flash up in a sweep of headlights.

He's home.

He gets out the taxi. His hand is enormous, bound like a mummy's in white gauze.

'Okay?'

He nods.

'Look.' You point up at the roof but the taxi and its lights are gone.

He can't see what you're looking at.

'*Look.*' You point at the darkest patch of the dark.

She moves.

He sees.

Together, you stare up at her, jumping each time she stumbles and scuffles.

You can't climb up there in the dark and the dew, and you can't wake your neighbours at this hour. If they're hearing any of this (how could they not?) you know that they'll think, 'It's just another bloody possum'.

There is nothing to do except go to bed and hope that she'll still be there in the morning.

Ø

Back in bed, he snores while you half dream and half speculate that you'll find a pile of feathers on the nature strip in the morning. She'll be frozen solid. Or have broken bones. Or her eyes will be pecked out of her head.

At dawn, that same scuffling sound jerks you properly awake. Metallic scraping. Then there's a new kind of sound: *thup*, *thup*, *thup*, like a soft toy bouncing down steps.

You fall out of bed and run outside.

She's gone.

You scan the shadows of the roof.

She's gone, she's *gone*.

You damn yourself for not waiting with her.

A cluck. Her soft, rolling song.

Half hidden behind a tree branch, she sits where the lowest gutters of the roof meet at the corner of the house. She looks snug, as if a great hand picked her up and gently tucked her into the leaf litter.

You walk into your neighbour's yard so that you are standing underneath her.

She's wide awake. She cranes her head and looks down at you.

'Stay *put*,' you say, pointing a warning finger at her.

You return to your house and grab the stepladder from the repainted room. You come back and prop the ladder underneath her. She watches you climb up, unfazed, as if she's wondering where you've been because, don't you know she's got things she needs to do today?

Eye to eye, you study each other.

'Stupid thing,' you say.

She stares at you.

You offer her your hand.

She pecks lightly at your fingers.

Your skin is sore and dry and all scratched up.

You're not sure how to hold her. You've never held a chicken before. Birds have always seemed so fragile to you, so easy to break.

You span one hand over her tucked-in wings. You

slip your other hand under her breast. Your fingers sink into the cold sludge of the gutter, searching out her legs. You lift her up and pull her towards you, hugging her close. Carefully, you step backwards down the ladder. She is so, so light. As you walk home she twists her head around, looking up at you. You look down at her, laughing. 'Girl,' you whisper. 'My lovely idiot girl.'

She is so, so warm. Stupid, to have thought she'd freeze, as if the intricate press of her feathers were for looks alone. Gently, you snuggle your fingers into the folds under her wings. The fine bones of her feel bendy, as if she'd bounce right back into shape if you tried to crush her.

You carry her through the sleeping house. You stand for a moment in your bedroom doorway. He is still asleep. For a second, you see yourself throwing her up and into the room.

Why not frighten him awake with the news?

Instead, you carry her through the laundry, past the snoring curve of dog and out into the backyard. You open the coop and gently plop her next to her two sisters. They are awake with the dawn. They peck her roughly as she tries to settle in next to them. Who'd have known a chicken could look sheepish?

Though you've spent the night losing her, and the morning finding her, you only hesitate for a second. Then, you open the coop's door again. Out the three of them tumble, strutting into the morning glitter of a new day.

Ø

Back inside, you go to your repainted room. Carefully, you open the taped-up door. You turn on the light. The newness of it hits you. It was right to go to the trouble, just in case.

You get out of your dew-damp pyjamas. You wash your hands and your face and your muddy bare feet. You climb back into bed.

'Hey,' you whisper, shaking him. 'She's okay.'

But he is still sleeping off the drink and the hurt and the shock.

You turn away from him. He rolls over to you, just as he always does. Though your hands and feet are freezing, he pulls you close, tucking you in to the warm crook of himself. He drapes a heavy arm over your waist and, gently, gently, you place his wounded, swaddled hand over the cool bare skin of your stomach.

EAT. SHIT. DIE.

Now George, that idiot at Agápe's, might have been a crap cook, but he was onto something when he forced his muck down me each night and said, Leo! Eat up! If you don't eat, you don't shit. If you don't shit, you die! Suddenly thought of him at the club last night, while Bryce and Nina and Renee banged on about their alienation as creative artists and so on. The usual spiel. Another night lost to blah-blahs. Then, the inevitable boasting about who'd screwed who since last time. Renee won, as usual. She loves beating us boys. She loves rubbing Nina's fat face in it. She finally got with the red-headed chick from the café, and the thalidomider from the studio, the one with the pierced stumps who paints with his feet. I was too busy nursing my juicy, cramping guts to really listen but when finally, solemn as a saint, Renee led the usual closing sermon on how everything comes down to the universal, elemental, fundamental sex drive, I just wanted to scream, What are you *talking* about?

If you don't eat, you don't shit. If you don't shit, you die.

If you don't eat, you don't shit. If you don't shit, you die.

When your guts are broke you realise pretty quick what's fundamental. Eating. Shitting. I don't know about dying, except that it's like sex: there's too much written about it and it's all crap.

Time someone wrote about what really matters.

Time someone wrote about shit.

Ø

Nina, you eat too much. Every meal you tell yourself, You've *got* to stop eating like this. You never feel hungry. You never feel full. You're always out of control. Now it's 9pm. Again, you've sent yourself to bed to stop yourself eating. Again, you can't sleep: all you can think about is food.

Maybe Glen's right: you've overstretched your stomach. How does he put it? You're like Dr Who's TARDIS. Tard-arse, he says. Tard-arse lard-arse. Or you're like Mary Poppins' handbag, your guts looping around inside you without limit or end. He says you're a walking, talking black hole. That you could swallow stars. That you're a star's graveyard. He's getting very cosmic about your condition. There's no metaphor, he says, astronomical enough to explain where all that food goes. I could have done my thesis on you, he says. A new physics: Arsetronomy!

Well, of course you haven't defied physics. Energy is *always* conserved, and last week he caught you arranging your stomach around the table—with your hands—as if it was an annoying object that was getting in your way. The shame! Worse, the realisation: it *was* an annoying object that was getting in your way! Since then you've noticed how your fleshy armpits pinch and pull when you reach for things, and how when you drop something you just peer helplessly at the floor, distrusting your body's turgid hinges. A few nights ago, when Glen was in his room schmooping on the phone to Sally, you set up the bathroom scales. You filled a bucket with seven kilos of water: the weight you've gained these past few months. You told yourself, That's fat, Nina, blobbing through your blood, plugging your heart, exploding you slowly—a slo-mo super-duper-nova. You lifted the bucket: it was heavy! How disgusting, to pour such muck into yourself. How exhausting, to carry such weight around with you, all the time, *all* the time.

I'm getting in my way! you cried to Glen last night, as you shared the feast you'd cooked him because it was his birthday and he was missing Sally badly. Look, sis, he said, you know the deal. Energy in—he stuffed in another mouthful—must be equal to, or less than, energy out. He leaned over as if to fart. You didn't laugh. He stopped fooling. He patted your arm. It's just flab,

Nina. Just food. Accept yourself, or change yourself, but stop obsessing 'cos you're driving me *nuts*. He went back to his dinner, muttering, What is *with* women and food? You found yourself travelling his words up, up, up into space. You looked down at the earth and you saw how its men never thought about food, beyond wanting it and eating it, while its women cooked and gorged and starved and vomited and cried, their food morphing into all sorts of strange things in their guts: thoughts, feelings, rituals. Glen burped you back to the table, demanding, Cake, woman! Of course you'd baked him one. Of course you ate the whole thing once he'd taken his slice and disappeared for some optical sex with poor Sally stuck in Wadeye.

Well, it's easy for Glen to lecture you, with his laddery ribs and his hoppery limbs and his horsey face, all bony plains and stretched skin. It's easy for him to reduce everything to rationality. He might be right— you've just got to get a *grip*—but what if he's wrong? Can physics really explain everything? Can it explain compulsion, this force that's not quite a thought or a feeling or an urge, but some sort of a cell-deep, primal call to just eat and eat and eat?

Oh, rubbish! It's not your flab getting in your way, Nina. It's not some profound ancestral memory dictating things. It's you. It's just *you*.

Once again, your nightly prayer and promise. Today was the last time. Please let tomorrow be a new day.

Ø

I've finally forced myself to see Gallows (to get to the bottom of it, ha ha). I'm sitting outside his surgery, thinking about shit and society. I started thinking about this years ago. I was at a supermarket checkout, waiting behind an old woman, when a voice yelled, Pwoar, something *stinks*! A fleshy slap. I turned and saw a boof-haired kid with brimming eyes and a finger-pegged nose. His mother kept thumping groceries onto the counter. I suddenly wondered if, in my dreamy stupor, I'd farted or burped. Maybe I had B.O. after a humid morning sweating and writing in days' old boxers. As I turned away, disgusted, a warming stench hit me. Mum—look! *Thump.* I went to check my shoes, and then I saw it. I stared at the pencil-thin ankles of the oldie in front of me: over her heel and smearing onto the floor was a slug of soft yellow shit.

The old woman seemed oblivious to the squalling kid and the retching air. In fact, with her pin curls and mint dress and tan handbag, she oozed refinement; pure refinement, except for the shit—her shit—spreading over the floor. The checkout chick carried on heroically, chatting away as people began to move around the edges of the store: a manager, a boy with a mop. Finally, the old dame counted out her coins, put her bags in her trolley and disappeared up the street with her head held high, her pearls shining and her shit streaking a trail behind her.

For a moment everything stopped, as if the building's very fabric knew that something profound had just happened. Then the checkout chick smiled and asked me to step back. The boy trundled the mop over and we all stood, quiet as a funeral congregation, as he scowled and swirled and smeared the shit into bleach-smelling nothingness. As I watched him I knew everyone except for the hollering kid was thinking, Did the old woman *know* what had happened? If she did, was she okay? If she didn't, would she be okay when she realised?

As I walked home that day, I wondered what I'd have done if it had been me. Irrationally, but definitely, I knew I'd have gone home and killed myself. Realising this, I began to think seriously about shit and society.

Ø

When you were little, food was a treat. On Thursday nights you and Glen paced the shiny pink lino of the supermarket's junk food aisle while your mum stormed off with the trolley. You each had a dollar to spend. Every time you chose something Glen would say, I dunno if I'd choose *that* one, Nina, so you never got what you wanted and always coveted what he got. At home you'd watch TV and play your silent weekly game of Losers Finish First. You always lost. Later, Glen would lie in bed with his sweet trophy propped on his pillow. Nina, he'd say, look. He'd go Mmmm-mmm, and lick and slurp and suck in a creepy way until you ran over and punched him, yelling for your mum, who said it served you right for being a pig. It's always been like that between you and Glen. You want to eat, he wants to compete. You scoff, he savours.

It wasn't just sweets that drove you. It was every food, every day. If you'd done your chores or walked Chompy, you got snacks or seconds at dinner. If you achieved good grades you won two chocolate bars on Thursday nights and none if you'd done poorly, which wasn't fair, because Glen was good at everything and you were good at nothing. On Sundays, you hustled for the weekly roast, your mum tossing it to whoever she deemed best behaved, or she'd tell you to buzz off and would sit on the back step—the picking place—tearing the juiciest shreds from the bones herself. If your dad scored the corpse, you and Glen would hang around like scrapyard dogs, poised to pick his pickings because he just didn't understand the art of stripping flesh from bone. Once, he tossed a carcass onto the grass to see what you'd do. Of course you fought for it, and the only thing weirder than that is the image of your dad sitting by as if it were perfectly normal for a man to treat his kids like hyenas at a zoo.

Yes, your parents subscribed to the Pavlovian school of child-rearing. Just as they used cheddar to make Chompy turn tricks, they trained you and Glen with chocolate and meat. But now, Nina, you're your own food-treat dealer. You're the only judge of whether you've been good, and there's nothing you won't reward, is there? At recess today you trotted to the café to celebrate getting your Year 9s into poetry. In the afternoon, you hosed down two horny Year 10s without sounding like a dried-up old hag, and you rewarded yourself with fish and chips at the train station. So why did you then stuff down all that pasta when you got home? And why did you eat the slab of cake that Glen brought back from work? *Slab*, not slice. You can still see the look on his face when he came in from Telephone Sally and saw that the cake was gone. He wasn't pissed-off silent. He was just … Say it, Nina. He—the closest person to you, the only one left—was disgusted. Disgusted by *you*. Now you've slunk off to bed early again, and you're blaming your parents—*dead* people?—for what you do. If it's their fault, Nina, then how come Glen isn't a porker too? If it's their fault, how come you've gotten so much worse just recently?

Again, your nightly prayer and promise. Today is the last time. *Please* let tomorrow be a new day.

Ø

'Stool Sample Kit'. I'd rather give Gallows my blood, my piss, my semen, my goddamn bone marrow than my shit. Doesn't matter that he's an old man and a doctor and won't even look at it. Doesn't matter that he asks people for shit a dozen times a day. It matters that he's going to read *my* shit, that he's going to read *me*. Bloody George. You eat to shit to live, he said, but I've been eating and shitting and, yes, I'm alive but I might just be dying too.

So here I am, at home, following instructions. First, defecate into a clean container: make sure you do not urinate. Ha! Some lab rat, somewhere, is gonna think I can't read: I've been pissing out my arse for weeks. Second, transfer a small amount of faeces into each specimen jar. Easier said than done. I look at the wooden spatula that came with the kit. Throw it aside. Go to the kitchen. Contemplate a straw. Settle for a spoon. Who'll know? Somehow, I'm having fun. It's not every day you get to play with your poop. It's not every day you learn that things like dignity and integrity aren't all they're cracked up to be, that maybe they're just ideas in your head because it's the integrity of the body—not *you*— that matters. Finally, I spoon the murk into the jars, seal them, and dump them into the bag Gallows gave me. It's bright yellow and stamped up and down with the sinister black sickles of the biohazard symbol. Faeces, stools, biohazards: even shit-testing kits can't name shit.

I don't know whether to walk or drive this bounty back to Gallows'. For the past few weeks I've hardly left the flat. Lucky I'm on sabbatical because I can't go anywhere, now, without getting strategic about toilets. The club's become impossible too. So busy. No privacy. People noticing. Even Renee looked twice when I arrived last time. I walked straight past her to the crapper. When I returned she was all over me, saying, Wow, Leo, you look *great*! as if I've been fat and ugly all these years and not known it. How'd you do it? she kept asking. She's forever trying to hone herself down to her bones. I discipline my body, she says, I discipline myself. I discipline myself, she says, I discipline my art. Maybe she's

73

right. She's the only one of us whose work's really gotten somewhere.

That was a weird night. I was spacing out while she and Bryce sparred over their 'open relationship', sparred because he's screwed no-one and she's fucked everyone. Then he started banging on about his show, saying it's flopped because he's a tall poppy who's truly creative because he confronts the conventional blah-blah. I just had to ask him how artified porn was anything but derivative. Artified porn? he squealed. *Derivative?* Renee pissed herself laughing. So *true*, Leo! Even Nina giggled in that snorty, goofy way of hers. Bloody Nina. She just kept peering into me that night. Otherwise, she held the floor for once, though maybe she just seemed to because I couldn't take my eyes off her huge freckly tits heaving in and out of that ridiculous black dress of hers. She always looks like a dog's breakfast—like she'd *eat* a dog's breakfast, Renee would say, like she'd eat a *dog*—but there I was eating her with my eyes and pretending to give a damn about her classes and her poems and her new—her first—publisher. She was so happy that Renee just had to cut in and cut her down, looking at her while commenting again on my *fantastic* weight loss. Of course, Nina shut right up and sat there, swamped by the fact of her fat.

Stupid Nina. And Renee, you shallow bitch, you'd be stunned if you saw me now: even Gallows stared when I walked into his office yesterday. He felt about my caving guts and jutting ribs and weighed me and ummed and ahhed and, though he never mentioned it, we were both thinking of the C-word as he handed me this shit-kit. And no, Renee—no, Bryce—we weren't thinking of cunts and cocks and cunnilingus, or convention-confronting creativity. We were thinking of that good old plot-moving, world-shaking crisis that gets everyone interested in a B-grade story: cancer, cancer, cancer.

Hell, I'll take the risk. I'll walk this stuff back to the doc's because I'm bone cold in here and it's burny bright out there and if that old woman could stride her shit down the street then I can flaunt my biohazards too. What have I to lose? I'm in Gallows' hands now.

Ø

You couldn't believe it when Leo appeared in the doorway of the clinic. Your insides tumbled: once, when you thought he'd seen you; then, when you saw that he hadn't; then again, when you saw the change in him. You've never seen anyone so thin. You've never seen him so beautiful.

He strolled across the waiting room, as bendy and bouncy as a blade of grass, swinging a plastic bag and whistling the jolliest tune you've ever heard. That was when your dread from the club forced itself to thought: Please, not my Leo! (*My* Leo? Look, there's another feeling morphing into thought. You must be insane, Nina. Leo stopped caring years ago. And why would he care now—now that you're as big as a whale?)

You know your dread-feeling for Leo is right

because his lightness hurled you straight back to that final sharp morning, years ago, when Eddie waltzed in and ate breakfast with you and kissed you and looked at you just as he used to. You'd thought everything had shifted into place. But no. Eddie had just worked it out: weight doesn't come from the past; it comes from the future. You weren't seeing things fixed. You were just seeing what a man looks like when that weight lifts off of him: within hours, Eddie was dead. At Dr Gallows', Leo looked just as floaty-free as Eddie had. Just as floaty-free.

You watched Leo give his bag to the nurse. When he turned to go, he suddenly saw you. He stopped whistling. He stared. That was when your insides really sickened: he was so freed up that he wasn't even mad, not like he normally is when you catch him off guard. He just hesitated, smiled, strolled over and said, Hey, Nina Boppalina, good to see ya. He just stood there, playing that stupid rhyming game you played at uni when you were both practising to be 'great writers', that game he dumped once you'd spent years writing nothing very great and going nowhere very far. Hey, Leo? you said, tripping over your own question mark. He shrugged, answering you with a jangle of his terrifying bones. Then you blurted, Come for a feedo, Leo Schmeo? Glen's away seeing Sally. For once, he wasn't all excuses. Indeed, a feed! was all he said. You rhymed up a time and he said, Cheerio, I gotta go, and tootled out the door.

Then you went in to Dr Gallows. You told him

you needed a check-up. He checked things up and said, You're obese. Lose weight. So then you asked him what you were *really* there to ask him. He looked at you as if you were stupid. He said, What do you mean you can't stop eating? Like an idiot you repeated, I can't stop eating. Like an idiot, he repeated, What do you mean you can't stop eating? You both sat there, staring at each other, baffled. Stop eating so much, he said, and exercise more.

Behind your sunnies you bawled all the way down to the café. There, you stopped crying, went inside, and ordered your usual—just as you knew you would, just as you knew you shouldn't. You sat in your favourite sun-drenched seat, loving and hating every sweet bite as you erased Dr Gallows' angry face behind lists and lists of what to cook for Leo, your Leo, coming to dinner next weeko.

Ø

Gallows was not happy. Nothing conclusive could be said about my shit. Nothing conclusive could be said about me. So now I'm in hospital getting ready for what they call a 'top and tail'. Sounds cute, but it's not, though the real agony lies in sitting across from this woman while she talks about how she's going to enter my anus and go down my throat and read me from the inside out. I came here to see a gastro guy, not this film-star beauty. I can't even look at her face.

Had a spectacular time on the shitter last night after

chugging the potion that Gallows gave me. To clean you out for tomorrow, he'd said, handing it over. Dab—don't wipe! He was trying to lighten things up, but he looked grey as he shrugged over my results and poked around my gutless guts. Later, as I surfed a tsunami of shit into the night, I thought of Renee and her detox diets and the million times I'd mocked her. You detox every time you shit, I'd say, every time you piss. But yesterday I wondered if she's been right all along: though my body's been purging itself for months, last night showed me that I'm still full of filth. As I watched it gush away from me I felt great, like I was cleaning myself right out of myself, and when I woke up this morning I felt sore and raw and newborn.

Stupid Renee! And stupid me for thinking she'd ever be right about anything because, after all, I'm still here, stuck in myself and squirming in front of this beautiful woman.

Weird, how I spent all last night worrying Renee or Bryce or somebody else would walk in on me. Later, as I lay in bed, waiting for the smaller waves to hit, I realised what a fool's fear that was, because no-one ever drops by and no-one ever will. No-one's seen me for ages. No-one except Nina, and Nina doesn't count. I might as well flush myself down the toilet for all the world cares. Realising this, I suddenly sensed them, all the people in the world who're exiled by their shit and piss and pain, and I wanted to scream, How the fuck do you live? and, What will happen to you? But then, when I asked myself those same questions, I found no answers. I guess there are just some things you've gotta live with, even if they stop you living.

The gastro girl stops talking. She leads me into her surgery and introduces me to the hunky guy who's going to shoot me up with the sleep-juice. He looks over me to make eyes at her, and it turns out I've got nothing on that old lady in the supermarket. I'm humiliated. I'm scared. I can't hold my head up high or look either of these two good-lookers in the eye. I thank God when a frumpy old nurse walks in. I focus on her lumpy back-side and watch her looping a long black hose over a silver hook. What's that for? I ask. You don't wanna know! she says. Everyone titters as the liquid sleep pulls me under.

Suddenly I'm awake and surrounded by chattering patients and a glorious symphony of farts. I realise the symphony is my own but I'm so relaxed that I don't care a damn. A nurse appears and asks, Okay luv? and I say, Great! and my arse says, Fart! She gets me dressed and leads me to a room full of armchairs and TVs and sits me near three cushiony old biddies. They smile at me, like I'm one of them. For the first time, panic swells in me. I focus on the TV. I watch some fatsoes confess their teary tales to Oprah. Then I remember Nina, sitting like a big pink pudding at Gallows'. I was walking on air that day, resigned to whatever fate Gallows was going to read from my shit. I think that's why I said yes to dinner: I thought I'd die first. (God, Nina annoys me. How she acts like she cares about everyone and everything.

I might be a selfish prick, but I don't see how caring about everything is so damned different to caring about nothing at all.)

The gastro girl appears next to me. She shrugs like Gallows: she's found nothing conclusive. She mentions the deadly C-word, but then she uses a new C-word and I'm caught on its curves and spikes: catabolic. That's *it*. That's what these past few days and months and years have been: catabolic. That what my whole *life* has been. Catabolic. *Catabolic*. I stare at the doc's smooth bare neck. I want to touch her, but before I can do anything so stupid, a miracle happens: *she* touches *me*. She strokes my hand as if she can sense the realisation uncurling in me: maybe I'll never touch, or be touched by, anyone ever again.

She asks me who's picking me up. My reply thuds onto the lino: No-one. She doesn't flinch. She smiles. Don't worry, Leo. I'll work things out. You're mine now, okay?

Ø

Leo sits across from you in Glen's seat. There's nothing to say. You don't ask him anything because he'll tell you when he wants to, if he wants to. Both of you eat and eat and eat. You hear him breathe and chew and swallow. You hear his cutlery tap against the plate. Only once do you ask, Is it okay? He nods, Mmmm-uh-uh. He doesn't look up.

After dinner he disappears to the bathroom. You go

out to the balcony. He's gone so long that you wonder if he's throwing everything up. You wonder if he's dropped dead. You turn to check on him. He's staring at you through the glass door. You stare back, feeling your thighs pour over your seat. Then he slides the door open, sidles around you, and lies down on Glen's yellow banana lounge.

Together you watch the white and red twinkle of the cars coming and going along the street. You offer him a cigarette, gesturing back to uni, when you each posed and pretended you were too cool to care that the world you wanted didn't want you. You can still feel the agony of that final year when he froze you out, as if he'd understood that cruel was the currency of cool in cliques like Bryce and Renee's. You'll never forget the first time you saw Renee with Leo. Saw how he looked at her while she looked through him. Saw how her perfect body and clever talk made you ugly and stupid. Saw how she—and she alone—knew how to sculpt self-knowledge into something magnificent: all that sex into stone; all her sex, all her stone. You and your stupid poems never stood a chance.

When you light your third cigarette, you look down at the street, and begin. You tell Leo everything he never bothered to ask you about. Then you tell him about Glen and his work, and about light and dark and time and space and weightlessness. You tell him how your poetry and Glen's physics are really one and the same, for you're both just dealers in metaphor, and isn't everyone just trying to put a shape on things? And you tell him, too, how you must move out soon: not because Glen has asked you to, but because you know he can't.

When you finish, you look up. Under the harsh fluoro of the street lamp Leo looks just as a man should on a banana lounge: starchy and stringy and white. You want to laugh. But instead, fury surges through you, roiled up by thoughts that you know—now—you will never say aloud: I *hate* you, Leo, for forgetting me, for ignoring me, for mocking me and for never *ever* asking me how it's been.

You turn back to the red and white constellations of the cars. You say, I can't stop eating. You repeat yourself—just as you did at Gallows'—as if Leo can't see what everyone sees when they look at you, weigh you up, and then turn away from you forever.

Eventually Leo puts out his hand. He only wants another cigarette. He leans in to your lighter, muttering, Oh well. He lies back and says, I can't stop shitting. Then you hear it. It rumbles up from deep within him, up and up, setting his plastic cradle creaking, and it's not the pig in him that's laughing, it's him, it's *him*.

Ø

I could stay like this forever, full of her food, looking and listening and wondering if she'll let me dress my bones in her, warm myself in her, rest in her. Look at those big, sad cow's eyes, sizing me up, looking to see if I hear her and see her. I have. And I do.

Nina, I know you'll be gentle, that you'll make a ritual of it, that you'll make a feast of me, that you'll relish me, that you'll pick my bones till they're so damn white we'll throw the light right back at those precious stars of yours. Together, we'll blind the lot of them: Glen, Gallows, Bryce, Renee and Georgie-boy. We'll show them there's a thousand ways to eat and shit and live and die.

THE WISHED FOR

ENTER FROM THE gate. A weatherboard house. Hard red borders slashed everywhere: the window frames, the eaves, the doors and the door frames. The smell of fresh paint, even at the gate. This smell of fresh paint from the darkening red and bright new cream, glaring between blood borders. Pass through the drying garden: see how its edges merge into the forest. Notice the pot plants: geraniums, succulents, paper-petalled daisies; plants that find it easier to live, than to die. Approach the wraparound veranda. See a huge wooden wheel propped—stopped—between the wall and the weather. Next to the wheel, a door. A front door? A back door? From the outside, look in: a kitchen. Wooden benches, wooden floors, wooden everything: a patchwork crafted from trees that took centuries to grow, days to chop down, and months to twist into this house where—after all—just a handful of lives have unfolded.

Ø

She stands at the sink, peeling potatoes. She wears a shapeless cotton dress. Her arms and legs and feet are bare and her hair is pulled back roughly. Her forearms are starched with freckles, but all she sees is the violent action of her hand. How well peeler and wrist burst skin off potato, cell off cell, insides from outsides. How useful a thing it is, this peeler of skin. She wonders who invented it. Wonders when, and how. Wonders why she wonders such things and, wondering this, stops.

She looks out the window. The bits and pieces of her just-begun garden dwindle into the trees, which spread into the distance, blanketing the mountains. In places, the canopy thins and disappears. Through these key-holes she sees lawns of ferns: the forest under the forest. Stopped, and staring, she waits for the slow shift in atmosphere, from the sharp-wet sounds of her peeling, to her breath-held pause, to the cacophony outside, filtering in: the cackle and caw and bell-ring of a million birds; the relentless drum of the cicadas; and the rough music of the wind, picking things up, shaking them about, throwing them down again.

She peels four potatoes. Walks across the kitchen. Reaches for a pot hanging from a hook. Dashes salt into its base. Fills it with water. Puts it on the stove. Lifts the potatoes from the sink. Carries them to the pot, drops them in. Stands next to the stove till the water boils. Takes a fork and rushes it across the foaming surface. Stares down at the potatoes, naked and stupid, on the steel base. Puts on the lid.

Back at the sink, she cleans out the peels: one sopping handful. She holds her dripping hand away from her dress, opens the door, walks across the veranda and around to the side of the house. With her free hand, she lifts the lid off the compost bin. Averts her face from the hot uprush of stench. Throws the scraps in. Returns the lid. Waits for the pungent oily haze of eucalyptus to seep back in from the forest that grows and rots all around. Then, the headache of fumes from the scorched paint.

This smell of fresh paint, she thinks. These smells of compost, gum trees, and sun-burnt dirt. Are they all it takes to string a life together across time? These things that never change? These constant things, that pull into the present all that has been attached to them in the past?

An upsurge of nausea. She covers her mouth. Memories flit across her mind like ghosts, like birds; like words lost on the tip of a tongue.

Suddenly, a low, soft noise.

She stops. Does not move. Does not breathe.

Something padding through the scrub?

Something there?

For long seconds her ears try to pick out the problem: nothing.

She makes herself go over to the bushes. Looks. Waits. Listens.

But there is nothing to see.

There is nothing there.

She returns to the veranda. Walks to the kitchen door. Opens it. Hesitates in the doorway, her back turned to the outside.

Ø

She wanders down the track that leads to the main road. She passes the stuck and rusting gate: half open, half shut. The lowering sun warms her neck. By the time she eats her dinner, the light will be yellow, and everything else will morph into those golden shades and softer textures she'd always imagined. Strange, how this place felt so familiar when she discovered it, just months ago. It was as if her lifelong daydreams were based on something other than the vaguest of wishes. To have a place of her own, somewhere. A place far away, somewhere. A place, somewhere—anywhere—full of plants and animals, and free of people.

But she never imagined this heat: stifling, inescapable, dangerous. Never imagined this hard white light glaring off everything. Never knew of the stretching quality of time, or how the present and the future are always woven with threads from the past. Never predicted the itch and burn of the sore little absences she unwittingly created in that final act of leaving.

Well, she won't dwell on all that. She can't.

Huge ferns line each side of the track like a guard of honour. Her faded dress, the sticky mess of her hair, and the sweat trickling behind her knees feel like a defiant but ill-judged statement against the ferns' regal presence.

Her feet are bare, but her thickened soles hardly register the trail's sharp multitude of sticks and stones. As she walks further from the house, the ferns press in closer, forming a cool, shadowed corridor. She trails her fingers over the black, thatched bristles of their ancient bodies, then stops before one of them. Looks up, for a moment, at the tapestry of light and dark that interlocks its fronds. Then she is pushing her fingers deeply into the trunk's fur.

A thrill of fear.

Is this what men feel when they cross such boundaries, with—or without—permission?

How different it is to be the one who enters, who intrudes.

Her mind flutters backwards, but stops short as her fingers reach the fern's body. There is only roughness and hardness there. Just roughness, and hardness. No explanation of how these plants so persistently, so elegantly, succeed in their project of living.

She continues down the track. Its edges are overgrown with creepers and runners and weeds. With her heel, she scuffs up any plant that attempts to grow on the path, then she squats down and flicks it into the scrub: a warning. As she does this, she pictures the cleared yellow moat that surrounds her house. Feels here—as she does there—how the forest watches and waits. Waits for the tracks and roads cut into its belly to crumble. Waits for the buildings and the old left-about machinery to break down or burn up. Waits for the living wires laced through its canopy to break, disconnect, die. Waits for the orchards of alien trees to disappear under its relentless growth. Waits, really, for the wounds that people keep inflicting upon it to heal over.

Well, the forest will have to wait a little longer. She's here now, and she has already painted and planted her battle cry.

She plucks out another weed. Flicks it to the side. Walks on.

She smells the boiling tar before she sees it. Then suddenly before her—stretching from left to right—is that immutable slick of black.

As she steps onto the road, she hears it.

Just like before: something in the shrubbery.

There it is again, to her left, near the letterbox. *Snap*. Silence.

A shuffle. A rustle.

Fear pounds her heart into her head. Her breathing stops, hooked in her throat.

She can't look.

She must look.

Slowly, she turns her back to the road. Looks down the trail. Scans the forest on either side. Feels a tension resisting hers.

It can see me, she thinks. It can see me.

Crack. A branch flies at her—right at her.

It thuds to the ground. She looks down at its splintered end, lying flush with her toes and the road's shoulder, its foliage streaming back into the fernery. It is huge.

Heavy enough to have split her skull.

She stares at it. Sees, again, the strangeness of its movement. How it flew across space at her, like a spear. How it flew *across* space, like an arrow shot from a bow.

Impossible.

It simply broke and plummeted straight down from above: a typical widowmaker. That's all it did, and a gust of wind moved it strangely. That's what happened.

But out here, by the wide and silent road, there's barely a breeze. There are just walls of heat, shimmering up from the tar into the white-hot sky.

She stretches her minutes, waiting, watching.

But there is nothing to hear.

Nothing to see.

Ø

The kitchen: steam filled and clattering. She rushes to the pot. Volcanic white blotches erupt from under its lid and slide down its sides. A glutinous puddle grows on the stovetop. She pushes the pot off the gas flame. Slowly, the kitchen returns to its usual quiet.

She stands before the stove, looking at the mess. She must have taken longer than she thought she would. She tries to recall what it was that she did, what it was that took so long. But she can think of nothing. She sees the letter, fat and inevitable, at the side of the sink. Must have dumped it there, rushing for the pot. Yes. It is the letter that she got from the letterbox. The letterbox that sits by the road. The road that she stood on during the scare in the scrub. The scare that happened after touching the fern, and before that branch nearly killed her. That all happened, just now.

She looks down at her arms, crossed tightly in front of her. Yes. She remembers seeing this very dress when she looked down at the branch at her feet. That all happened today.

She looks again at the stovetop. Sees that the gas is turned to its highest setting. She turns it off. Goes and sits at the kitchen table. Stares at the stove from across the room.

Didn't she leave the gas set to low, as she always does? She can't remember. Every day she peels four potatoes and puts them to boil slowly while she checks the letterbox. Every day she does this, and so she cannot distinguish one day from another. Did she turn the heat down today, as she should have?

She shakes her head. Shakes it hard.

Of course she didn't! Who would have turned it up?

Her chest shudders. A strange sound fills the room, then darts away again. It takes her a second to understand. For as long as she's been here, she has not laughed aloud like this. Hasn't she said a single word? Can this be right? It must be right. She tries to say something—to see if she recognises her voice; to see if she still knows how to speak—but she can think of nothing to say and so she just sits there, stupidly shy and silent.

She stands up then, forgetting why it was that she sat down. She gets a dishcloth and picks up the pot. She skews the lid to one side and tips the milky water into the sink. The steam rushes up over her hands: too hot. Quickly, she drops the pot back onto the stove. Gets the milk and butter and cheese out of the fridge. Measures these into the pot. Salt. Pepper. She roughly mashes it all together. Puts on the lid to let the flavours melt and meld. Remembers, again, the letter by the sink.

She picks it up. She studies her handwritten address. It's been blurred, a little, by the potato water. She notes the postage stuck in the corner: twice as many stamps as needed. Turns the envelope over. On the back, the sender's address, carefully printed, with the state and country underlined, as if it has been sent from a different state, from a different country. Scrawled at the bottom, a phone number and an email address.

So many details.

She weighs the letter in her hand.

Not her details.

She replaces the letter next to the sink. Returns to her pot. Lifts the lid. Inhales the buttery steam. Gets a plate and a fork. Piles the mash onto her plate and goes to the door. She opens it and sits on the splintery steps of the veranda. The plate is warm on her knees. The light is warm too, making everything look flushed and distinct, as if each blade and leaf and petal is striving to catch the last of the sun's rays. This is her favourite part of the day. There's no weight, now, of empty hours stretching ahead of her, threatening to be wasted. There's the purposefulness of cooking, of making something whole from beginning to end. And then there's the best bit, this bit: eating whilst countless plants and animals shift into their evening poses all around her. Every single day works up to this point.

With reluctance, and a small flutter of panic, she finishes her dinner.

All that was vivid and rich with depth, a moment ago, is suddenly flat and grey. She stands. Carries her plate and cutlery to the door. Steps inside. As she closes the door behind her, her thumb pauses over the lock.

After all these months, she still hesitates. Still scans the shadowed garden for shapes and movements that she does not recognise.

But there is nothing to see.

There is nothing there.

Ø

The kettle squeals. She makes her tea. Ignores the letter. Takes her mug and a book to the big kitchen table.

Every night when she sits to read like this, the rest of the day rushes at her, begging for the same attention she is about to give to the pages in front of her. Tonight, unwelcomed, the memory of her fingers sinking into rough, dark fur. The horror of a huge branch flying at her. The simple fact of a pot boiling over in an empty house. The image of an unopened letter, sitting by a sink. Tonight and every night—unwelcome, unwanted—the image of a woman reading alone in a house that is nothing more than a speck of light in an endless stretch of forested night.

She turns away from these images. Looks up at the windows. Watches the bugs throw themselves against the panes like confetti: the dusty patter of huge moths, the silent blur of tiny flies, the leggy silhouettes of huntsmen. She closes her eyes for a moment. Listens to their soft music. Once this sound frightened her. Now it comforts her; keeps her company.

For hours, then, she reads. She notes onto lined paper what she notices: things she understands; things she needs to understand better; things she's never known. Once or twice she gets up, wanders the house. Goes to the toilet, washes her face. Looks closely at her skin in the mirror. Drifts into the bedroom. Turns on the lamp. Makes up the bed so that it is ready and waiting for her. She returns to her book. Sits. Continues to read. Suddenly, as so often happens, something leaps at her from the pages. She underlines the text with the tip of her finger. Mouths the phrases to herself. Then, in big pressed-in capitals, she copies down the words that have slapped her awake. She sits back, stares at the truth on the page. Leans forward again, pen in hand, and circles the words. And again she circles them, as if, one day, she might need reminding that these notes mattered. As if, one day, she might do something other than file these notes away in a box, in a cupboard, in another room.

Soon, her mind begins to wander. She realises she is re-reading the same few sentences. Her eyes hurt. She puts down her pen. Looks over at the swarms throwing themselves at the glass. Walks over to study them. She is never sure whether she should leave the lights on for them. Never sure if darkness will spoil their fun, or grant them relief. Tonight, she turns the lights off. Then she stands and listens as their quiet music slowly fades away. She picks her way back across the moonlit room. Takes her mug and puts it in the sink with the rest of the day's dirty dishes. She won't clean them now. She'll leave them for tomorrow morning. How else can she connect one day to another?

As she turns away from the sink, she notices the letter. She is pleased at how well, for a while, she'd forgotten it. She picks it up. Tilts it towards the windows. Looks at the familiar writing. Again, she weighs the letter in her hand. Feels the promise that awaits inside: pages and pages, written just for her.

Of course she will not open it. For the moment that she does, his eyes—their eyes—will roll into the palm of her hand, and he and his tribe will stare at her with their hurt and confused goodwill.

Of course she will not open it. For the moment that she does, his voice—their voices—will fill her head, fill this home, fill the forest. They will ask her to share, to give, to take. They will talk and talk and talk. They will ask her to be a part of—the heart of—their life. To be a wife, a daughter, a sister, an aunt. A mother.

They will ask, Why? Why *not*?

But they will never listen for answers.

She looks out into the night-cast garden. Gazes, for

a while, at the only answer she could find.

She weighs his letter in her hand. Of course she will not open it.

This place is for the anonymous. The unnamed and un-naming. The un-speaking and unspeakable.

She opens the back door. Wanders to the compost bin. Removes the lid. Rips the letter up and throws it into the bin's dark guts. She takes the lid to the water tank. Upturns it under the tap. Fills it with water. Carries it back to the bin. Tips the water in. Returns to the tank. Refills the lid, returns to the bin, tips the water in. And again. Then again. Finally, she looks down. Searches for the white shredded paper in the rotting black.

But there is nothing to see.

There is nothing there.

Ø

Watch from the gate. Look at the weatherboard house: colourless in the starlight, blank in the moonlight. Watch as its windows darken. Feel it settle into the cleared space she has forced around it.

Snap a branch. Rattle a window. Cry out into the still summer's night.

Feel the house brace. Feel the forest's warm, rich air electrify.

See one of the rooms light up. See her, naked. See her startle at her sudden reflection in the night-mirrored windows.

Watch her walk from room to room: turning on lights,

looking behind doors, in cupboards and under beds. On she goes, stopping, listening, checking, moving on.

When she cannot sleep, when her mind assaults her, when a strange sound teases her, this is what she does.

When her daydreams mock her, or her nightmares shake her, this is what she does.

She searches.

Searches for nothing.

Makes sure that nothing, no-one, is there.

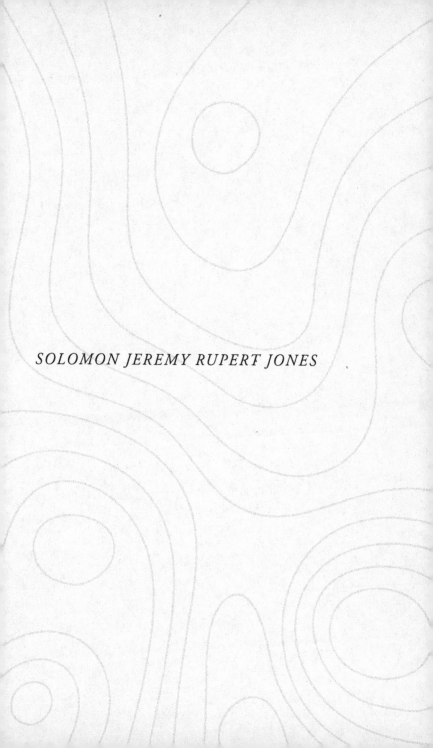

SOLOMON JEREMY RUPERT JONES

SOLOMON IS PREGNANT with paunch. He's budding breasts, and though he supposes it's time he stopped eating like a teen, he'd rather be stuffed than starving. Kate is as tiny as she was at school. Kate isn't into food. Kate's into winning and sex. She's always kicking people's arses at work, and she's always whipping Solomon's arse in bed. Since the end of high school he's obliged her fantasies, her favourite seeing her bony white legs grip his waist like pincers, while she grabs his hair with one hand and thwacks his butt with the other. Their bareback rodeos used to make Solomon feel, in every respect, as big as a horse, like a manly man—a horny, brawny beast—and he would bray and buck around their house, aroused by her arousal, desiring her desire, while she yodelled up a storm of smut that surged them towards sex so savage he was scared he'd break her little bones.

At Solomon's thirtieth, a decade ago, he got a card telling him it was time to Stop Aspiring and Start Accepting. Another card told him he'd Stopped Growing and Started Dying. He'd immediately sensed the truth of the first card, but the second card seemed arbitrary and morbid. Now, Solomon knows the wisdom of both cards, for his night-time romps with Kate are battering him to death. Now that he's more man than Manimal—a nickname she growled up that first time she clawed him into her—and Kate's legs struggle to grip his growing belly, her feet fly about, whacking his gut and arms and thighs and jaw as he canters half-heartedly around the house. While she delights in the new hazards of her gripless rodeo—especially the ever-changing acoustics of his ballooning backside—Solomon has had enough. He's exhausted by her inexhaustibility, by her drive forward, by her hunger to win, to race to the top, to reach the end, to set the fireworks sparking. Being both pathologically energetic and sans penis, Kate just can't understand that when a guy feels more like a hefty hoary hippo than a hot horny horse, he has trouble getting it up. The last time she flew in from work in a frustrated rage and demanded he Debrief her, he'd confessed he felt sleepy and fat and ugly. He'd whinged, Can't we just have *normal* sex for once? She'd rolled her eyes. Feeling reckless, he'd tried, Can't we just … *cuddle*? Disgusted, she'd straddled him—blocking his view of the TV—and said, Look Solly, you've gotta get your shit together. You know I'm up for anything, but quit it with this lazy, vain shame shit. He'd nodded: he *was* lazy and vain and ashamed. Then she'd turned a thousand saucy tricks to get things going, and soon she was screaming like a banshee as he—for once—got to ride her.

He'd felt happy afterwards: he still had it in him! And Kate looked happy too: Nice old-school moves, Solly! But as he lay beside her and listened to her deep, regular breathing, he began to feel all chewed up and spat out. He eventually dragged himself from bed, scrounged around the kitchen and then plonked himself in front of another late-night movie. As he stuffed down his cold and slimy butter chicken and tore at his rubbery naan, he wondered if he was a Life Partner or a walking talking dildo. He wondered what was wrong with him because he'd listened to a thousand guys at work grumble about their women Closing Up Shop on them Forever. He wondered if he loved Kate less. Then he wondered if she loved him less, though he doubted it. When Kate said a thing was true, it was true. When she decided a thing, it was decided. And when she promised a thing—like loving him Forever And Ever, Amen—it was promised. As he stuffed down his last bit of bread, Solomon tried to swallow the guilt that surged up in him as he wondered if he and she—their Royal We, their Happily Ever After—was going to be enough for him after all.

Ø

Solomon and Rob eat lunch in the staffroom. Rob is an Iron Man, and when he isn't policing dodgy insurance claims he's policing everyone's Life Style Choices. Listen Boss, Rob says, you've only got one body. You gotta respect it. Solomon munches salty peanuts and watches Rob plough through a stinking pile of green stuff. Nut fat is *good* fat! Solomon says, flicking a nut at Rob's head. Rob ducks and jabs his fork at the food wrappers piled at Solomon's elbow. Fat is fat, man. When they return to the office, Rob stops at Regine's cubicle. When Regine isn't accounting for the firm, she's a personal trainer, accounting for—as she calls them—Fat-Fuckers. She's also studying dietetics so she can get out of insurance and Make A Million from the Goldmine that is the Di-abesity Epidemic. Solomon offers Regine his nuts. Rob giggles, then asks Regine about Good Fat and Bad Fat. Regine ignores Solomon's nuts, looks pointedly at his chins, and declares: Fat is *fat*.

Later that day, there's cake for Gloria's sixtieth. Everyone is enjoying it except Gloria—who's on another diet—and Regine and Rob, who Never Eat Junk. Yum-yum, Solomon says, making eyes at them as he takes an enormous, luscious bite. He thinks of Kate that morning, pinching his hairy breasts and calling him her Bu-Bu-Boomba on her way out the door. He'd suddenly asked her if she minded his growing girth. She'd paused mid-flight, turned, and then put down her briefcase. She took a good hard look at him, as if she hadn't looked at him properly for years—which maybe she hasn't—and said, Oh, you've always been Supersized Solly to me. And you were a real *prick* when you went all Hunky Gym Junkie. As usual, Kate's right: he was born sumo sized. In his early thirties, when he suspected his proportions were stopping him climbing the company's sleekly styled corporate ladder, he dedicated himself to Self-Improvement. Sure enough, within a few years he was Sexy And Successful. But he was also miserable: he'd realised that every promotion he got simply unveiled another promotion he should get. He was sick of chasing rainbows, and he was sick of living by the credos No Pain Means No Gain and Hunger Is Your Friend, because no pain *clearly* gained no pain, and—goddamn it!—hunger is *nobody's* friend! Being an All-Or-Nothing kind of guy, he relieved himself of guarding himself from himself, and signed his body over to Fate: If fate is fat, he proclaimed, so be it!

As Solomon moves in for another slice, he hears a yell. It's Gloria, galloping at him from across the room, bellowing, To hell with it! In unison Rob and Regine yell, Don't do it, Gloria! Solomon hands her a slice. They stand there, side by side, stuffing their faces and grinning at each other. Suddenly, Sofia Khoury Condello materialises between them. She playfully bumps Gloria's bulging bum with her own gravity-defying derrière. Gloria forces a tooth-gapped, chocolatey smile and then—cake demolished—descends into her inevitable lament about her Failure and her Weakness. Don't *worry*, Sofia says, handing Gloria another slice. My ma was like me—she could eat whatever she wanted. Then she hit her thirties and everything fell down and ballooned out. Now she's Fat As A Whale. Sofia arcs her arms and puffs her cheeks like a blowfish. It's just *natural*, she says. Everyone cringes on Gloria's whale-sized, puffy-faced behalf. Sofia guffaws and tucks into her cake, rolling her kohled eyes and moaning with pleasure. Oh God, she says, this is *so* good. Regine glares at her, then glares at Rob, who's entranced by Sofia's high-gloss, cream-laden lips. I can't *wait*, Sofia says, till I'm hitched, 'cos then I can sit back, have a stack of kids and let everything *go*—just like *you*, Gloria! Horrified gasps puncture the air. Oblivious as ever, Sofia bolts down the rest of her slice, whips out her diamanté-encased phone and pronounces, Baby news! Regine makes gagging gestures and disappears out the door. Everyone else follows except Solomon and Gloria: they want more cake. As he eats, Solomon studies the photo of Sofia's newborn niece. He eats and stares and begins to feel lightheaded. He's not sure if he's woozing because he's taking off on a sugar high or because he's struggling to comprehend that the tiny, skinned goblin he's looking at is a brand-new human—a brand-new human that some woman has grown inside of her and then pushed out into the world as gruesomely as a beast in the wild. He suddenly feels sick and thrusts the phone back at Sofia, who yelps at the time and hurries back to reception.

It's not until he's having dinner with Kate that Solomon realises Sofia's niece has been on his mind all afternoon. Kate stops eating. She stares at him. She stands up. She points her knife at his face. What the *fuck* is going on, Solomon Jones? Solomon shields himself and races over the last few minutes of their conversation, searching for his crime. You've been babbling about babies for *months*. What's the fucking deal, Sol? Silence, then, as Solomon realises she's right. He's been thinking about babies *a lot*. In her lawyer's voice, she goes on, You *said* you didn't want kids, right? We *agreed*, didn't we? And it's true. They agreed a long time ago that dogs, kids and in-laws weren't on the cards. Don't give me this shit *now*, she says. I've thrown all my eggs in your basket! Kate shakes off her mistake. You know what I mean, you *shithead*! And he knows she's right because she's thirty-nine and she's made a life with him and she's only ever been honest with him about everything. I'm *sorry*, he yelps, as she throws her knife and fork at his head. I'm sorry, he yelps again, as she sizes up the wine bottle, though it's hardly his fault that his brain or his cock or his past or his future has called his loins into a queasy quiver of baby-making. Because that's what this restlessness in him must be about, right? Because that's where this growing sense of yearning must be coming from, *right*? What are you, Solomon Jones? she screams. A bloody *woman*?

Later, in bed, after hours of fake-sleeping, Kate whispers, Don't you love me anymore? Of course I love you! he says, and of course it's true, and of course it's a lie, because his I Love You has acquired—just as he has—an unignorably ginormous But.

Ø

After that night, Kate begins to sleep in the spare room. The morning coffees he makes her, and the evening meals he cooks her, are all left to go cold on the kitchen bench. When their paths cross in the house, she tiptoes around him like he's a stinking turd, and she ignores all his spoken, post-it-noted, emailed, voicemailed and texted pleas to Talk It Over. They've been together for a very long time, so Kate is very good at pissing him off—and hurting him—and if he weren't so sure that this fight cut a different and deeper nerve than all their others, he'd have done what he usually does when she stonewalls him, which is to haul her kicking and screaming into the bedroom, throw her over his knees, pull down her knickers and spank her tiny backside until she laughs her head off. On the seventh night, Solomon is wondering if this Old Chestnut is worth a try, but as he rouses himself to find out, his phone goes off: Kate has finally replied—through the wall—to one of his texts. And so, on the eighth night, Solomon sits in St Germaine's, looking out into the rain-drenched street, waiting for her to arrive.

When she comes in she glances at him, then looks away again. Head down, she walks across the restaurant, then sits silently across from him and stares at her hands, clasped together on the tablecloth. It's the first time he's had a proper look at her all week. She lets him look. Lets him see that she's not just Pissed Off, not just being a Sulky Bitch, a Stroppy Cow, a Pain In The Arse. She's something else altogether. She looks old and ashen. All pinchy and flinchy. It takes him a moment to find the right word. She looks ... defeated. He realises that, if someone can lose a game by refusing to play then Kate is, for once, The Biggest Loser. Instinctively, he takes her hands and pulls her towards him. He cups her face and leans in close, hovering there, smelling her lips and her rain-sprinkled skin. Then he kisses her slowly and fully on the mouth, in just the same way he kissed her for the first time on their last day of school, when he knew it was his final chance to let her know that she was the girl for him. I'm sorry, he says. She looks up. He watches hope flash across her face. Watches it flit away again as she realises his I'm Sorry is really an I'm Sorry *But*. Another Big But. He's full of Big Buts these days. She slumps back into her chair.

Solomon begins to say all the things he knows he shouldn't. Katie, he says. She frowns at her hands. *Don't* call me that. Sorry, he says. Kate, doesn't *any* part of you wonder what it'd be like? Red blotches creep up her neck, over her cheeks and into her hair. Are you deaf? she says. Are you blind? Are you stupid? Clearly, he is deaf and blind and stupid because he repeats his question, though this time he avoids her flaming face and looks out into the sparkling dark. No, she says, I *never* wonder. Don't you think, he goes on, that when you're old, you'll wish you'd had them? No. Aren't you curious to meet them? Who? Our kids. We don't have kids. You know what I mean. No, I don't. And still, he goes on. Aren't you curious what it'd be like to have a baby? Kate searches his face, her own a strange mix of anger and sadness that he has never seen before. It's easy to want a baby, Solly, when you're not the one who has to have it.

Well, what can he say to that?

Cast away on their little island of misery, they sit in the golden light of St Germaine's and let the French muzak and the chattering laughter block out the silence straining back and forth between them. How, Solomon wonders, do these so-called Natural and Fundamental things get so damn complicated? There's no point musing upon this aloud, for he knows what Kate will say. Fuck *Nature*! Dying of cancer is Natural! Lynch mobs are Natural! Raping and being fucking raped are Natural! Don't you hoon about in your goddamn BMW, Sol, with your decaf lattes and your iPad and your anti-depressants and then lecture me about what Nature Intended!

Suddenly, Kate leans back in her chair and crosses her arms. She cocks her head and appraises Solomon with her coolest diamond-standard lawyer's glare, the kind she uses to slice and dice witnesses and crims and jurors and even the judges themselves. Promise me now, she says, that you'll answer me truthfully. Though Solomon's promises clearly aren't worth shit, he nods. Is there Someone Else? Is Someone *Else* making you think all of this, all of a sudden? Solomon thanks God, then, that he doesn't have to lie because no, there isn't Someone Else (is there?). It just came from nowhere, he says. It just bubbled up from *nowhere*, he says. Then he starts laughing, relieved that there isn't Someone Else (is there?), and he says, You're right Kate, I *am* worse than a bloody woman! Kate's face flashes white, then creases and crumbles, and she begins to cry and cry and cry. All alone on the other side of the table, Kate wails like the baby she refuses to have.

Kate's not practiced at crying. She chokes and snorts and coughs. Her face is swollen and a snail's trail of snot shines from her nose to her ear. The other customers look up and shuffle about and try to keep talking. They glance at Kate and they stare at Solomon—hard—like he's A Bastard. When Kate finally stops, as abruptly as she began, she looks at him and then looks stupidly around the room. She sees everyone staring and she yells, Oh, go *fuck* yourselves! Everyone rustles nervously and glares at her like she's A Crazy Bitch. The waiters move in, sharpening their whispers. Kate stands. The waiters pause. Everyone inhales as she stares Solomon down: What do you mean you're *worse than a woman*? Solomon squirms. Kate says, You think I'm not a Real Woman, not a Natural Woman—as your motherfucking mother would say—'cos I won't shit out your kids for you? (You'd never know, from the way she talks, that Kate's a top-notch silk.) Solomon flinches. The restaurant flinches. From the corner of the room someone mutters, Ouch! Someone else chimes in with, Yikes! Someone else giggles. Solomon hears himself saying, No, no, *no*, but even as he says this a part of him is yelling, Yes, yes, yes, yes, *yes*. Kate seems to hear this part of him. She pulls all five feet of her tiny self up and proclaims: Solomon Jones, I will *not* be the reason you don't have children. I will leave you. I will buy you out of the house. Seeing as you've fucked everything up— you Lying Son-Of-A-Bitch—I will keep what I want and you can have what's left. She puts a hand on her hip. She juts her small breasts out the open front of her trench coat. Then she tosses her beautiful long red hair over her shoulder, as if showing him—for the last time—what A Fine Piece Of Womanly Ass he's losing.

She strides to the door. Stops. Turns. Storms back at him. She leans down so her face is only centimetres from his, and says, You're full of *shit*, Solly. I always *knew* you were full of shit, but I thought it was honest, decent, normal *man*-shit. She straightens herself up again. But you're just full of *shit*-shit, Solomon Jones. Shit-shit, she repeats, nodding, as if she's just explained everything to herself. She belts her jacket tightly. She turns and strides back across the restaurant, flipping the bird at the corner from which another series of drunken Ouches! Yikes! and giggles sound. She slams out into the rain-sloshed street and then, quite simply, she is gone.

Ø

As Solomon and Kate divvy up property, visit banks, sign off documents and have one quick and final hug—a hug where vertigo rushes through him, glorious and sickening—Solomon notices that a part of his brain has broken free and is kicking about his head, sneering that he's Insane and he's a Real Prick because people aren't clothes that you can just try on and wear in and then chuck away for something new just because you feel like it. But *she's* leaving *me*! Solomon replies, though he and Wussy Pants (as he's named the rogue) both know that the only reason he didn't leave Kate was because he's exactly what she said he was: lazy, vain and ashamed.

Now that he's facing Singledom, Solomon confronts his nude and rude reflection each morning. He runs his hands over his hairy breasts and his round and rosy nipples, and recites, Solomon Jones, what's past is passed! Now's your chance to *really* Remake Yourself, Find Your True Self and Embrace Your Future! Wussy Pants ponces about his head, mimicking him and sniggering about Self-Help, New-Age, American-Style Bullshit. Solomon flexes his bingo wings and tells Wussy Pants to, Shut Up! and, Watch Out! because Solomon Jeremy Rupert Jones is going to Live The Life That Only He Can Live! Wussy Pants wheels about laughing, yelling that Super-sized Solly had better watch out that he doesn't end up living the life that only he *deserves*.

Within seconds of their split, Solomon watches himself get Unfriended on Facebook at a spectacular rate. Apparently their friends are actually Kate's friends, and they all think he has Sucked Her Ovaries Dry and Abandoned Her. He shrugs off this public condemnation and wonders what Kate thinks of these so-called friends, because if they knew her, they'd know that she's no pushover and that one of her more extreme beliefs is that Women With Brains Should Be Mandatorily Sterilised. What really bothers Solomon, though, is how his own mates and family seem to have jumped on the same damning bandwagon as Kate's friends. Apparently everyone is an expert on his Shituation. One night, over beer, Gav tells him, Sol, Kate's *hot*. She's smart and she's funny and she's got *balls*. What the *fuck* are you doing? Solomon babbles something about something. Gav shrugs and says, You're free to *what*? Man, I've been living on Lonely Street *forever* and it's fucking *shit*. I'd cut my *dick* off for what you two had. Solomon cringes, and again babbles something about something. Sounds like a load of *crap*, man. Solomon hasn't seen Gav for a while. Solomon's mother is furious. You've known each other since you were *babies*! You can't just walk away from that kind of history. God, you're all the same, you bloody men with your bloody dicks! And *every* woman wants kids, even if she doesn't know it. Solomon doesn't ask how he's meant to have kids with a woman who doesn't know she wants them, and instead lets her rant about how he's not getting younger, and he's not getting any better looking, and he never *was* good-looking, and did he know that when he was born she'd checked his name tag because he'd looked like a monkey's miscarriage and *all* of her babies had been beautiful until she'd had *him*? Losers Can't Be Choosers, Solomon! Solomon hasn't seen his mum for a while either, and he douses Wussy Pants in beer each time he gleefully applauds these knee-buckling lectures.

Solomon used to drive in and out of his garage and never knew, or cared, who the hell his neighbours were, but now that his new place is on the tram line, he hardly uses his car. For the first time he knows the names of everyone in his street, and they know he has a name other than That Fat Guy. He begins taking long walks after work to explore the suburb he's lived in—and ignored—for twenty years, and to distract himself from Wussy Pants' merciless attempts to sabotage his search for his True Self: though it's been six months, Solomon's True Self still eludes him. (Illudes, Wussy Pants mocks. *Illudes*, idiot!) Solomon also hopes his wanderings will help curb his gut which, though he damns the shallow world for the fact, may well obstruct his attempt to meet someone new. His walks and talks have taught him some amazing facts about his suburb. Did you know, he tells Gloria and Sofia and Regine, that I just happen to live in *the* Lesbian Hub of Melbourne? *Four* of them live in my street! Have you heard of the Brethren? Man, those kooky-kooks are spreading like gangrene! Did you know there's *three* brothels on High Street? Regine snickers, How'd you find *that* out, Boss? She snickers again when he tells them about his favourite new café, The Pumping Pumpkin. For Sofia and Gloria's benefit, he details all the mothers' groups' conversations he's overheard in there, where women compete about who's prolapsed or haemorrhaged or lost all feeling in their nipples. He recounts their arguments about the Right Way to give birth and raise babies, including a screaming match over the teachings of some nature-knows-best-guru-gyno called Lionel Vaginal. That fight didn't end until one woman jumped on her chair, grabbed her apparently Still-Intact-Vag and yelled across the café: Heil Caesar, *bitches*!

Regine points out that lesbians and mad mummies probably aren't the best candidates for prospective mates. Sofia points out that guys who hang around women and kids look like perverts and usually are. Solomon waves them off, joking that lesbians always need sperm donors, and new mums are perfect because they're obviously fertile and at least half of them will get divorced sooner or later. Anyhow, he says, thinking of Cowgirl Kate, Some women *like* perverts. Some women *are* perverts. That's when Gloria says, What about Sofia? Sofia *loves* losers, crooks, creeps and pervs! Sofia shrugs helplessly: she can't deny it. The combination of her striking Euro-Middle-Eastern-Somewhere-Or-Other good looks, the fact that scummy guys have been in her milieu for so long, and the fact that her parents have never made a secret of regretting their pile of daughters—all five of them born in the pursuit of a son—has seen Sofia set her romantic bar very, very low.

Hmmmm? Gloria says, her drawn-on eyebrows jiggling as she looks from Sofia to Solomon to Regine. Regine stomps out of the room in protest: if there's anything more disgusting than fat people it's the idea of them having sex with thin people, and compared to Solomon, Sofia is a rake. Hmmmm? Gloria says again, nodding in excitement as Sofia stands, and begins to walk around Solomon, pursing her luscious lips and appraising him like a prize bull. Solomon can practically hear her ticking off a very short, very unambitious list of requirements in her head. Alive? Tick. Adult? Tick. Male? Tick. That's *it*—that's her list! Or so he hopes. Well, she says, kneading her chin like a thoughtful stockman, I've been out with Anglos before, and I've been with a fatty or two, too. Solomon burns, though he's not sure if it's because she's calling him fat or because her smoky eyes have just stripped him bare. She finally stops circling him and declares, But I've never been with a Fat Anglo before!

That's how it begins, and forever after Gloria will take credit for getting Solomon The Best Breasts In The West.

Ø

They start like children. Chaste, embarrassed and excited, they go on daytime weekend dates. Solomon takes Sofia to The Pumping Pumpkin, so the staff and regulars can see that he's not the creep they seem to think he is. Weirdly, they just look at him *more* askance when they see him with her. He ignores them, and sallies bravely forth in his courtship, doing with Sofia all the things that Kate would never waste her precious time on: people-watching in trendy cafés; wandering aimlessly through the botanic gardens and the zoo; taking ferry rides and train rides and bus rides to places neither of them have ever been before. Sofia drags him to monstrous suburban shopping centres, hauls him to day spas, and takes him to huge multiplex cinemas where they watch chick flicks and get all touchy-feely before wandering—squinty eyed and disoriented—back into the sunlit street. Sofia loves the thousands of tiny things Solomon delights her with, and can hardly believe he doesn't expect instant repayment in the form of Hand Jobs and Blow Jobs and Quick Fucks. Solomon delights in how easily delighted she is, and—used to Kate dissecting and judging everything he's ever said even as he says it—he adores how Sofia listens to him and how she seeks his opinion on everything. When he catches her reciting those opinions as if they are her own, he tells himself he is infinitely more charmed than he is disturbed.

Everything seems to be going swimmingly until one afternoon when Sofia interrupts Solomon mid-sentence, and tells him she's Sick Of Bullshit. She tells him she wants the Real Deal, because if she doesn't get married—*subito!*—she might just let her parents marry her off to one of her cousins in one of the Old Countries. She's turning twenty-eight, which is lucky for *him*, she says, because her family doesn't care *who* she marries anymore, so long as some man—even a fat, old Anglo atheist—gets her Off The Streets. Solomon flinches, but only a little, and promises her that he understands and agrees: No more Bullshit! Real Deal, or No Deal! He tells himself to be happy. He's getting what he wants, right? And the conventional and traditional choices are

Time Tested And True, *right*? He hears Kate yelling out the very long list of Terrible Things that tradition and convention have sanctioned for thousands of years. He ignores her, and he ignores Wussy Pants who reminds him that he *was* the Bullshit in a *real* Real Deal.

Soon after that confrontation, Solomon makes the big move of asking Sofia out to a Romantic Dinner at a fancy-schmancy restaurant. This is their first night-time date and their first time out drinking. They shuck and suck oysters, and joke about aphrodisiacs. Sofia has never had oysters. She says they taste like boogers. Solomon asks her how she knows what boogers taste like. She burns and he admires her burning in the candlelight. A little later, a little drunker, Sofia strips a lobster and tells Solomon he has to stop eating so much junk or he'll ruin his semen. They giggle at the word semen. Later, and even drunker, Solomon cracks open Sofia's strawberry brûlée with a sharp tap of his teaspoon, and tells her she'd better be faithful or she'll get chlamydia and her womb will fall out of her vagina. They giggle at the word vagina. Then Sofia asks him, seriously, if that's what happens when you get chlamydia. He's not sure, and he tells her how all of Australia's koalas are dying of chlamydia too. There's a lull in their conversation as they wonder what all of this means.

The posh people in the restaurant sneak glances at them and wonder how such an Old Pig ended up with such a Young Hottie. But then they look closer and notice Sofia's clothes are cheap and shiny and her makeup is overdone and her beautiful hair is really a crazy, curly, glitter-drenched mess. They see that Solomon is much younger than they first thought and that, though he's huge, his clothes are fitted and flashy, and his shoes and his watch cost just as much as their own. They murmur unkind things about Escorts and Prostitutes, Viagra and Rogaine, Rich Sleazebags and Cheap Suburban Sluts. Solomon and Sofia gaze at each other, ignoring the censorious sea that swirls around them and—just as Solomon had hoped—they are soon tumbling home to his place.

Half-drunk, they fumble through the front door and straight up to his bedroom. He points out the new pot plant he's placed by the bed: To honour you! A madonna lily! He rustles the plant's elegant satiny leaves. I'm no virgin, Olly! Sofia laughs. Neither's Madonna! he yelps, sensing her nerves from across the room. To avoid contagion, he gets busy with music. Sofia reclines on the bed, fully dressed, shoes on. She watches him, one hand lying on her stomach, the other absently stroking the lily's leaves. Eventually, he comes over and sits next to her. They look at each other, suddenly shy. She raises her face. He kisses her. Not at all sure what's expected of him, and therefore moving slowly, he begins to undress her. All the while she keeps playing with the lily. When he's stripped her down to her underwear—all black lace and white ribbons; all French-Maidy-Whorey; all of it chosen, he realises, just for him—Sofia suddenly flicks off the lamp.

Solomon stops. He's never had sex in the dark before—not by choice. He doesn't know what this means. He's suddenly acutely aware of his own sweating bulk next to her statuesque beauty. He pulls back from her. He says, We don't have to do this, Sofia. Not if you don't want to. In the darkness, he finds her broad, flat stomach and strokes it. She's so soft, so warm. Oh yes, she says. We *do* have to do this. He senses her reaching through the black. Feels her hands clasp behind his neck. She pulls his face down to hers. Kisses him. He kisses her, and forgets about the light and the dark and begins, instead, to feel his way around her and inside her, struck by surprise at how very, very different she feels and tastes and smells to Kate.

But really, what did he expect?

Ø

So now they are A Couple. Everyone is both amused and disturbed at the sight of them as they try—and fail—to ignore each other in the office. Relationships between staff are discouraged and relationships between senior men and junior women are seen to be Bad News, at best, and Illegal, at worst. With much elbow-nudging, and jokes about *Personal* Training, Rob boasts to Solomon how he and Regine finally Hooked Up in the gym toilets. It's 'cos of *you*, man! I should've known you'd have the *guts*! Gloria also claims that Solomon's romantic success has inspired her unprecedented affair with a married greybeard from upstairs: If *you* could get *Sofia*, she tells him, I figured Geoffrey'd be a cinch! Even Gav musters up enough goodwill to congratulate him. Fuck Sol, Gav slurs, as pissed and depressed as ever, I dunno know how you fuckin' pulled *this* off, man. She's fuckin' *gorgeous* and *sweet* as pie. She could have any guy she wants, man. You must have some kinda weird ... *pheromones*, or something. I just don't fuckin' *get* it. Solomon's mother is ecstatic that her new kind-of-daughter-in-law is young, prays at the church of marriage and kids *and* Christianity, and shows her the kind of Automatic Respect that Kate always refused to. You're blessed, Solomon. I don't know what she sees in you, but you've gotten her *somehow*, so don't mess it up! Solomon takes these comments in the spirit they are intended—he's a Lucky Boy—and tries to ignore Wussy Pants' delight in what appears to be the general consensus that he's Highly Undesirable.

The real proof that the world has recognised their Official Coupledom comes in the mail, in the form of an invitation to Kate's fortieth. Somehow, Kate has found out about them, and she and her New Guy—whoever *that* is—have done the Grown-Up Thing and invited them to her birthday. When Solomon shows Sofia the shiny gilt invitation, they stare silently at the strange asymmetry of the names upon it: Solomon Jeremy Rupert Jones & Sofia Khoury Condello scrawled lightly beneath the hard black typeset print of Fabien Dubois & Kate Jones. For the millionth time, Sofia wonders aloud at the strange coincidence of the matching surnames.

For the millionth time, Solomon plays dumb, ignores the question that Sofia is asking-without-asking—Why didn't he marry Kate?—and explains how they simply became friends after being repeatedly paired for classroom exercises because of their proximity on the classroom role. Solomon jokes that, had there been more or less students, or a different alphabetical mix, he might have ended up sharing his bed with Bazza Jones-Murray for twenty years, and Kate might have ended up sharing hers with Miranda Johnson. Imagine that, ha ha ha! Sofia does not laugh. Instead, she looks at Solomon for a very long time, as if trying to work something out.

When Sofia isn't around, Solomon finds himself drifting over to the fridge where the invitation is trapped under a big magnetic banana. He stares at the four names' strangeness and wonders what Love has to do with things. He pictures Kate riding him like he's a stallion, and then pictures Sofia in bed each night, wide awake and tense with waiting, and he wonders what Sex has to do with things too. It only took him a few weeks to realise that something other than Urgent Passion made Sofia squeeze and push and porno-talk him during sex. He realised she was well practised in the art of Doing Her Duty and Getting It Over And Done With As Quickly As Possible. He realised he'd become Sofia's sexual chore, just as Kate's bareback rodeo riding had become his. Wussy Pants finds all of this, of course, *hilarious*: How green's the grass, buddy? Solomon wants to ask Sofia what's wrong—if there's anything he can do, or if she'd rather do nothing—but before he can, she opens and closes the subject herself. One night—after three minutes of ball-busting, back-scratching, supersonic sex—she whispers, Sorry, into the darkness. He says, What for? She doesn't reply, because they both know what for. He hugs her. He says, Don't worry. Then he hears himself say, I love you, Sofia. He spoons her, and hopes like hell he's telling the truth. They lie like this for a while, till she says, Do you *really* want kids, Solomon? Yes, he says, though his response sounds just as strange, to him, as his I Love You. You know, she says, I've wanted kids since I *was* a kid, Olly. How weird is *that*?

When Sofia is finally snoring away—for, as lovely as she is by day, she snores and farts like an old man all night long—Solomon disentangles himself. He wanders to the fridge, opens the door, and gazes inside. He feels Wussy Pants staring over his shoulder into the bright whiteness. Why's your head always in here, buddy? What're you looking for? Your True Self? Solomon ignores the bastard. Closes the fridge. Opens the freezer. Stares inside. *Does* he love Sofia? *Does* he want kids? He grabs a tub of peanut butter ice-cream. Hears Kate laughing at him, as she used to in her cheeky-kinky, utterly relentless way: You and your beloved *penis* butter ice-cream, Solly! Hears Wussy Pants leer at him: Did you find what you're looking for, *mate*? A tub of somethin', or just a tub of *anythin*'? Fuck off, Solomon mutters. Fuck off, fuck off, fuck off. He gets a spoon, sinks himself into the couch, and flicks on the TV. Sweet relief: a rerun of Baywatch. He sits back and tries to sedate himself with shovel after shovel of salty sweetness, and scene after mind-numbing scene of D-grade, E-cup entertainment. As he watches Pamela Anderson's boobs volley-ball around the beach, he concludes that Sofia must be right: everything *is* weird. How can Kate love sex so much but puke at the idea of kids? How can Sofia loathe sex so much but want kids more than anything else in the world? He wonders if Kate is right too: that there *is* no such thing as Natural. Then he wonders if Kate isn't quite right: it's more that there's just no such thing as *un*natural. Then he wonders if anyone is ever right or wrong about anything. And if anyone is ever right or wrong for anyone. Or if everyone is always right and always wrong for everyone always.

Ø

Solomon and Sofia sit in his car and stare out at the huge Victorian terrace. It looks colonial—like something a Brit would build in India—and sits right across the road from the beach.

Gosh! Sofia squeaks. Golly gosh, Solomon mutters. For minutes they sit there looking at the New Guy's house in stunned silence. Finally, Sofia tugs Solomon's sleeve and says, C'mon Olly, let's knock 'em dead! But she remains frozen to her leather seat, looking as shiny-eyed and shit-scared as when he took her to meet his mother. Let's go! he says, hoping like hell she'll demand a retreat. But she doesn't, and soon they stand, hand in hand, on the tessellated tiles of the front porch. When Sofia presses the big golden bell, panic twists in Solomon's throat. He wants to go, he *must* go, but he can't go because he knows that, if he does, Sofia will think it's because he's ashamed of her. Wussy Pants snarls about inside of him: *You* ashamed of *her*? You're a selfish prick, Solomon Jones. You're an *idiot*! And, for once, Solomon agrees. He *is* a selfish prick because, standing here and shrivelling like a salted slug, he's forgotten—*again*—that this party must be a hundred times scarier for her than it is for him.

He'd only realised Sofia was terrified when he'd watched her getting dressed. As she flustered about in front of the mirror—Is red too Slut Whore? Is black too Uptight Bitch?—he'd recognised that she was dressing for Kate and for Kate alone. Only then did he remember Sofia's eye-bulging silences each time they'd seen Kate yelling at rallies on the TV, or heard her screaming down dissenters on the radio, or read her eloquent damnations in her weekly newspaper column. Only then did he truly realise that, to Sofia—and to most people— Kate wasn't the fourteen-year-old foster-kid tomboy that *he* saw, but a glamorous and terrifyingly powerful Somebody. Suddenly, all of Sofia's jokes about being a Dumb High School Drop-Out, about being a Gold-Digging Western Suburbs Wog—about being A Nobody—didn't seem like jokes at all. Watching Sofia run around in her underwear—G-string or bloomers? Push 'em up or let 'em swing?—all flushed faced and swearing, he finally saw what Sofia had seen as soon as he'd opened the invitation: tonight, they were going to Meet Their Makers. Who *cares* what people think? Solomon yells silently at the whole damn world. *Everyone* cares what people think! Wussy Pants hoots back, laughing his head off.

Suddenly they hear footsteps tapping towards the door. Quickly, Solomon bear hugs Sofia, kisses her, pinches her big round bum and declares, over her squeal: I can't *wait* to show you off tonight! A smile breaks through her shit-scared face, then disappears as the door swings open and the New Guy stands before them. Solomon doesn't know what he expected, but he didn't expect this. The New Guy is as short as a jockey, but what he lacks in stature he makes up for in brawn: he looks like a pit bull—a pit bull in an exquisitely tailored tux. He has a square chin, thick silver hair, and curiously smooth, luminous orange skin. With a sudden and bitter satisfaction, Solomon decides that the New Guy looks like a Plastic-Fantastic, LA-styled Oompa Loompa—on steroids. The New Guy bares his perfectly straight white teeth. Then he raises himself up onto his tippy-toes, kisses Sofia on each cheek and pronounces her Beautiful! He speaks with the rounded vowels of the Eastern Suburbs—exactly the kind of accent Kate used to impersonate at dinner parties when parodying her friends and foes from court. Sofia blushes and gushes. The New Guy shakes Solomon's hand with both of his own—using that corporate handshake that Solomon himself uses when he needs to falsify sincerity and authority—and stares up into Solomon's eyes as if he knows who he is. Solomon stares straight back, realising that the New Guy probably knows *exactly* who he is. His jaw clenches on the thought. He forces a smile and steers Sofia quickly into the cool, dark hall and wonders who's showing what off to whom tonight.

Inside, the terrace turns into a brightly lit white box. It's Uber-Modern, all glass and steel, all minimalist except for the taxidermied exotic animals that are posed all over the place. Impossibly, a full-grown giraffe stands by the glass staircase, its head rising up into the second storey. A bonobo hangs off a chandelier—frozen mid-swing—and a flamingo is poised on one foot by the back door, gazing longingly at the swimming pool. As Solomon begins to imagine Kate and the New Guy riding the animals and each other—a midget version of Jane and Tarzan—Sofia grabs him and begins to drag him around the room. For Kate's Sake, all of his Ex-Friends are pretending to be Old Friends for the night. At first, Sofia seems unaware of the sneers behind their smiles, but Solomon soon realises she's on a mission to douse their scalding looks with bucketloads of booze. Within an hour she's graduated from wine to mixers to shots. Then she starts sniffing around for coke—They *are* lawyers aren't they?—until a *ding ding ding* sounds across the room.

Everyone stops. The New Guy suddenly appears, climbing halfway up the staircase. He waits for silence.

Then he turns and looks up the stairs. Everyone follows his gaze. There she is! Kate descends slowly and awkwardly. She looks embarrassed, but she's laughing, clearly finding fun in the New Guy's apparent request that she make a Grand Entrance. She's dressed in a puffy pink frou-frou dress, all bows and ribbons and ruffles. She looks like she's wrapped herself up as a present. This woman—the queen of flats, army boots and runners—is wearing six-inch *heels*? Solomon feels a deep and nauseating pang: she looks *so* familiar; she looks *so* strange. What the hell is he even doing here?

Kate totters down the stairs and stops just below the New Guy so that she is eye level with him. My lovely Katie, he says, then pauses—dramatically—looking over his shoulder so that everyone begins to clap. Solomon feels himself blinking stupidly. *Katie?* Whenever *he* used that name she'd hunt him down, because *she* knew that *he* knew that her feckless bastard of a father used to call her that before he chucked her into the human garbage bin of Child Protection. The New Guy turns fully to the crowd, holding Kate's hand, and begins to tell the story of how they met (Saving The World, hotel stays, working long nights, wink-wink, nudge-nudge, blah-blah-blah). Then he goes all voice-crackly. He's Emotional. He looks at Kate for a long time, then he turns back to the room and yells, We're getting *married*!

Silence. The New Guy's smile falters. Kate frowns, then she hollers: I'm fucking *forty*! She thrusts up her champagne glass. Finally—thank Christ—the room erupts into applause and yelling, but even as people congratulate them, Solomon senses stunned pockets of silence and hears, between these pockets, stutters of muttering. What the ...? But she ...? Because anyone who knows Kate knows that she's as Pro-Marriage as she is Pro-Life. Numb and stupid and slow, Solomon feels himself beam at Kate and the New Guy. He sees his hand raise a glass to them. From a great distance, he watches them raise their glasses in return. The New Guy smiles right at him, looking very happy and very relieved. Kate also looks right at him, but Solomon can't tell if she's smiling or wincing. She shrugs, looks away. Solomon feels his Ex-Friends watching all of this. He's sure they're thinking exactly what Wussy Pants is screaming: Take *that*, you Bastard! Slowly, he senses Sofia looking at him. Her eyes are bloodshot. She looks confused. She says, But I thought— —. Solomon wakes up and yanks her out into the backyard.

Later, when they get separated in the mingling, Solomon heads straight to the darkest corner of the garden. Between the lap pool and the back fence, and behind a palm tree, Solomon finds a huge stone hippopotamus to sit on. Its head stretches out over the bright blue water, as if it is drinking. Solomon sits side-saddle on its back, and watches the party. Soon, Kate appears at the door. She is barefoot and has changed from her fairy-floss dress into the red silk slip she bought decades ago, on their Big Trip to China. He still remembers how he'd told her to get the white—for she always looks best in white—and she'd scoffed at him for being an Ignoramus: White's for *dead* people here. Solomon slides further back on the hippo, but Kate's looking for him, and she knows him, and she spots him. Within seconds she's walking his way. Hiding? she says, pulling back a palm frond so she can see his face. He shrugs at her, just as she shrugged at him on the stairs. She notes the impersonation and lets the frond go, flicking him in the face. Ow! he says, covering his stinging cheek. She ducks under the plant and climbs onto the hippo so that she's sitting in front of him, facing away from him, straddling the beast like she used to straddle him.

They sit quietly for a while, then she says, Looks like I finally made it to Partner. Solomon doesn't reply. He can't see her face and so he can't read her tone at all. Is she being sarcastic? Funny? Is she talking about work, or the New Guy? Both? Suddenly, her shoulders slump. I meant to tell you, Solly, she whispers. I just didn't know how. After a moment, her arms begin to move. She's stroking the hippo's head. He watches her, then hears the whiny voice of a pathetic kid come out of his mouth— the voice of a kid they both knew a long, long time ago. You never wanted to marry *me*, Kate. She doesn't hesitate. You never asked me to marry you, Solomon. This is true. It's also true that she never asked him to marry her, either. And that he knew her thoughts on The Institution. And that he therefore assumed getting married was never an option. He suddenly sees that he shouldn't have assumed any such thing at all. He could have asked her, anyway. He should have asked her, anyway.

Marriage matters to *him*, she says, nodding towards the house. It matters to him *a lot*.

Do *kids* matter to him too? Solomon whines. Was it just that you didn't want to marry *me*? Was it just that you didn't want *my* kids? And again, Kate doesn't hesitate. Last time I checked, Solomon, it was *me* who wasn't good enough—not providing enough—for *you*. She pauses. Resumes her stroking of the hippo's head though now she looks more like she's slapping it. You bloody well know (slap) what I think about marriage (slap). But what I *don't* like about it (slap) is much less than what he *does* like about it (slap). And what he likes about the *idea* of kids (slap) is much less than what he likes about the *reality* of me (slap). But I guess *you* (slap) wouldn't understand *that* (slap), now would you, Solomon? (Slap, slap, slap, slap, SLAP.)

He looks away from her sharp, jerking shoulder blades. They sit quietly for a while. Kate stops bashing up the hippo. They listen to the chat and laughter drifting over the pool. Solomon remembers St Germaine's— how their silence seemed to tug his heart to hers, hers to his. Now their silence has become two silences, shooting away from each of them like train tracks into the dark— forever close but never touching again, not ever, not ever.

What's this like? he asks, waving his hands around her head at the house and the pool and the hippo and the New Guy—who they can see through the plate-glass back wall. He's wearing a flowery apron over his tux, and is arranging pastries onto huge silver dishes. A toucan hangs off a chandelier above his head, swinging back and forth—somehow—as if it's alive. The New Guy suddenly stops and looks out past the flamingo into the garden. He's squinting, searching. Then he smiles and waves to a woman standing by the pool. The woman waves back and he returns to his work. Kate shrugs. It's just *different*, she says. He's like no-one else I know. She pauses. But then, Solly, so were *you*.

Were. Were. Were. Solomon can't move, can't speak. Even Wussy Pants halts in his ruthless, meddlesome roving—all of his smartarsery thumped out of him with this one mighty whack of the past tense.

Suddenly Kate says, I got rid of it. She half turns to him, so he can see her profile. I couldn't believe it had happened. You know how careful I am. I'm like Fort-fucking-Knox down there. She cranes around fully, awkwardly making eye contact with him over her shoulder. She's nodding and saying, But I wasn't going to be talked into *that* too. Solomon nods back at her and, when she asks, he promises he won't tell anyone whatever the hell it is she's just told him. She turns around, then leans back into him. He puts his arms around her bony little body and awkwardly—from his side-saddle position—pulls her close. He holds her tightly and pushes his face into her hair. Over twenty years of his life rush back at him with its smell. He pulls away sharply, but she pushes herself back into him, pulling his arms even more tightly around her, demanding this last embrace, this final, final hug.

Eventually—confused and hurting, and desperate to end this ending—Solomon croaks into Kate's ear, Am I still your Manimal? Always! she shrieks, laughing and flinging her arms up and back, hugging him clumsily from behind. He tries to laugh too, but instead emits a very loud squawk, a sound that makes everyone stop and peer into the pool-lit shadows. Inside, the New Guy registers the silence. Solomon and Kate watch as he looks out and then steps into the garden, his hands on his frilly floral hips. When he spots them, he shakes his head theatrically, then flounces back in to his pastries. Kate giggles. Everyone looks at her: a little baffled, a little shocked. As they slowly return to their chat—still casting glances—Kate sits up. Like I said, she whispers, he's just *so* different! She dismounts the hippo and turns to face Solomon properly. He's a brilliant lawyer, she says, but he's so fucking *straight* about some things—like The Sanctity Of Marriage—yet so damn wackadoodle about everything else. He makes a pilgrimage to Mardi Gras *and* the Vatican every year. And he's vain! He wears *lifts*, like *Stallone*! He has a tanning machine upstairs! He gets lipo and fillers and *Botox*! Kate beams. She looks as proud as a peacock and as happy as a clam, so what can Solomon do, other than smile—and try to escape?

He jumps off the hippo and begins to shuffle left and right. But Kate's not finished with him yet. She won't let him past. Well? she says, her smile dissolving as she nods across the pool at the Venus de Milo who stands on the other side, encircled by a group of slick-looking young men. She's beautiful, Solly. Sofia suddenly looks up and sees him. Automatically, she smiles. Automatically, he smiles back—till he realises that she is completely Off Her Face. Swiftly, then, he lifts Kate out of his way, just as he used to when they fought. He deposits her back on the hippo and walks the length of the pool towards Sofia, feeling—in his bespoke Zegna suit—like no-one less than James Bond. He stands outside the circle of men and coughs. They shoulder-shuffle him back, ignoring him until they see that she is looking at him with Pure Love. She's a Lamb To The Slaughter, Solomon thinks, taking her arm and pulling her away.

Oh puh-lease! she says, as she trips towards the house after him. He doesn't know what she's talking about. She pauses at the back door and stares hard at the flamingo, What the *hell*? she says. Then she steps inside and stares at the New Guy, who grins right back at her, clearly enamoured with her from the moment she entered his house. No doubt she's as exotic to him as the taxidermied animals he collects. Hey shorty! she drawls. Nice skirt! The New Guy giggles. Solomon keeps shuffling her along. Really, she mutters, when they reach the living room. Really, she says again, stopping under the giraffe and staring up at its huge stuffed cock. Woahhhh papa. She looks around at everyone. How much? she asks, her hands reaching towards them. *How much …?* Solomon pushes her on through the frozen menagerie. He yanks their jackets off their creepy monkey-hand hooks, and shoves her out the front door. She sways on the cold tiled puzzle. With some trouble, she turns to face him. She looks up at him with her smudgy, glittery eyes. Her kid's eyes. Those big, dark eyes that always seem to await an answer to a question she hasn't yet asked—or he hasn't yet heard.

She gags. She covers her mouth, but a spurt of vomit breaches her fingers and hits his chin and his chest. Her eyes round in horror. He says, Don't worry! He quickly cleans everything up with the nearest palm frond. He hauls her arm around his shoulders, hurries her down the steps and across the road to his car. He throws her in the back, gets in the front, and floors it.

As Solomon drives home, he glances at Sofia in the rear-view mirror. Half awake, she gazes out across the bay, to where his suburb—now their suburb—twinkles through the dark. As he crosses the bridge, her eyes suddenly meet his in the reflection. She sits up and leans forward. Reeking of perfume and booze and vomit, she says, I *get it*! Then she laughs, burps, keels over and starts snoring.

Solomon focuses on the road ahead and tries to ignore his pasty reflection flashing at him in the mirror as he speeds under the street lights. Tries to ignore this stupid sense of restless yearning that's plagued him these past few years—pulling him towards God knows what. He suddenly wishes he believed in something or someone greater than himself. That he had someone greater and kinder than Wussy Pants to turn to. Because then he could beg for help right now—now that he understands.

Then he could pray for help that he'll be good enough for her. Good enough for The Best Breasts In The West. Good enough for Sofia Khoury Condello who's never been with a Fat Anglo and who hates sex and loves kids and loves him—loves *him*—and looks forward to, one day, just letting everything go.

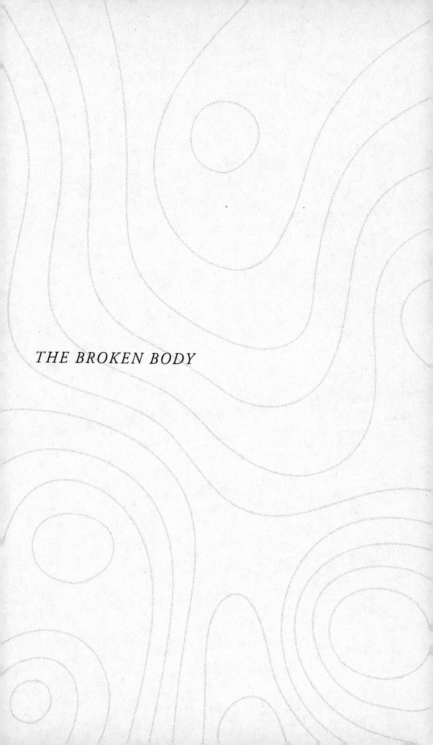

THE BROKEN BODY

As she swims each lap, she looks out through the fogged panes of glass into the lifting dark of the midwinter morning. She can see the refinery in full: it is miniature, centred perfectly in the metal-framed glass walls. A kilometre away, maybe two, it ghosts and glitters in a self-made steam of white. High above its cloud-spewing baths something ignites from steeples of steel. In the earliest hours of the morning, these flames will triple in size, lashing fire at the stars. All of this—these stretching geometries of light, these brutal balls of fire—gives her something to swim towards.

Ø

Slowly, her body moves backwards into the long steel tube. The blinding lights of the room disappear as she enters the tunnel. A humiliating drench of panic: the strip lighting along the tunnel's roof is only centimetres above her face. Just like the aisle lights in an aeroplane, she thinks, shutting her eyes. The lights that lead to safety when there's a crash. She tries to be wry and ironic, detached, crafting the analogy. She can't. She is in a coffin.

They told her not to worry, then they gave her a panic button. She clutches it hard against the knobbled plane between her breasts. She tries to relax, but her eyes and jaw keep clenching shut. She can't talk away the straitjacket of steel that surrounds her.

I can't sit up. I'm trapped. I'm trapped.

Blunt blasts of noise and, behind them, the heavy hum of massive magnets moving around her body, waves of energy stroking her insides.

Amazing, she thinks. Amazing, amazing, amazing. This is the mantra against panic she recited years ago, when a dentist drilled and hammered all of her wisdoms out of her head. 'Good girl,' he'd said. 'Good girl.' It *had* been amazing, being wide awake and without pain, but able to feel every heave and haul of bone as the man levered roots out of her jaw with garden-variety pliers. She'd gone home thrilled at her bravery, ecstatic, till she collapsed in bed vomiting bile-blackened blood, her mind suddenly assaulted by just-made horror-movie memories.

Now, she recognises that same panic. Realises it is not her own, but that of the skin and the bone: the terror of a body in danger. She could be a dog, a cow, a spider, a rat in a trap.

The radiographer, tired and indifferent (for she'd assured him that she wasn't claustrophobic), says: 'Not long now, hun.'

Gunshot of stutters. The *click*, *click*, *clicking* of a giant tongue.

Amazing, that this noise knows how to find a break in the bone, a tear in the tissue, a spill of stuff strangling nerves.

The machine's hum finally cools to silence. Her bed rolls back into the fluorescent room.

'Good girl,' the radiographer says. He leans over her, startled. 'Are you okay?'

She nods, horrified at the tears she can suddenly feel on her face and damp behind her ears.

He helps her wince to an upright position. Helps her off the table. He is gentle, but iron brands of pain sear her back, hips, legs.

'Okay?'

She nods, smiles.

Alone, struggling to dress, she cannot understand it. She is no longer trapped in the machine, but the animal-panic remains, pulsing through her. I'm trapped. I'm trapped.

No voice now, saying it will all end soon.

No panic button to press if it all gets too much.

Ø

Every morning she walks carefully down the cool tiles, rough-ridged against slipping. As she steps into the blue, she thinks: Here, I am beautiful. Here, we are all beautiful.

Amoebic memories awaken, joyful, pulling her under.

As the weight lifts from her body, the pain lifts too.

She was never taught to swim. The badly timed, rolling spit of her body leaves her breathing in bellies of chlorine. It's a triumph to freestyle from one end of the pool to the other, where she stops, sculling space. Then, breath restored, she struggles back again. Face down, she glimpses headless bodies moving all around her, everyone exposed in and enclosed by the same shared water. As intimate as sex, she thinks. As intimate as sex.

There's the squad swimmer in the fast lane, smoothed to Ken doll perfection by the water-light. There, in the slow lane, a huge woman bobs about like a boat, the dry-land wobble of her dimpled thighs and belly and breasts settled to a slow-motion grace: a barge's hull, bracing. There's the man whose loose skeins of black-haired skin signal a once-gross body. He turns a perfect pirouette at the end of each length. In the corner, a short stout woman cycles her legs into nothingness, the frills of her skirted swimsuit sighing around her like the wings of a manta ray.

She begins another lap, the last for today. In her lane, coming towards her, is the man whose dry-land hand flips and flops uselessly at the end of his arm. She hears it splashing the surface. From underneath, she watches the water meets his limp flesh. Watches the poor dead fingers resist, adapt, and then glide smoothly through the blue, a man-fin.

Always, this underwater watching reminds her of something she once saw on television: three elephants swimming across a lake. First, the camera shot them from above: stubbled heads breached the surface; ridiculous trunks spluttered for air. Then, they were filmed from below. The sun lit a twinkling halo around them, transforming each huge body into a silent, dancing silhouette. The camera moved upwards, tracing the water-smoothed wrinkles of their bellies and the slow rotation of their tree-trunk legs that, somehow, pushed them steadily along. Such clumsiness made graceful, such power turned gentle, tonnes of absurd design suddenly explained.

Standing up in the water, looking around, she knows it is true. Here, we are all beautiful.

She climbs out of the pool—one step, one step, one step—and back into a world of weight.

Ø

In Suite 101, a beige-suited man reclines in a high-backed leather chair. His hands are linked behind his head, cradling it. One ankle rests on a knee. His legs are spread wide open. He smiles at her. His eyes are the palest of greens, as cool as jade.

She stands on the other side of his desk. Smiles.

Tries not to look at the folds and creases of his expensively dressed crotch.

He gets up, shakes her hand and asks her to lie on the bed. He lifts her legs, one at a time. He checks her reflexes. He tells her to roll on her side. He lifts her skirt. He pricks a pin around her buttocks and lower back. 'Can you feel that?' he says. He pricks the pin around her inner thighs and labia. 'Can you feel that?'

He makes her get off the bed. Watches her tippy-toe around the room.

'Good,' he says. 'Good girl.'

He sits back at his desk and puts her MRI disc into his computer.

She watches his blank face as he studies her insides. What a portrait, she thinks, straightening her clothes.

She wanders to the wall furthest from the surgeon's desk. Here, dozens of children's drawings compete for space, shouting 'Thank you!' in rainbows of crayon and pencil and texta. There's a photo of a little boy with half his shining black hair shaved off. A long stretch of fresh and swollen stitches arc back from his brow. The boy grins.

She turns and sits at the other side of the surgeon's desk.

Finally, he looks up and shakes his head: a disappointed schoolteacher.

'Well,' he says. 'Well!' He casually slides something across the polished surface at her. It is cool and heavy and fits into the palm of her hand. It looks like

148

an elaborate door hinge: smoothed metal and moulded plastic; nuts and bolts.

He begins to explain. He makes a cutting gesture across his belly. He retrieves the object from her and pushes it into his imaginary gash. He jiggles the thing about, showing her where it would sit and how it would move.

'You'd get a bit of a scar.' He stretches two fingers taut across his gut. 'Same as from a caesarean.' He shrugs.

He leans back again: ankle on knee, legs wide, head cradled.

She does not know where to look. She directs her questions to the children's 'Thank you!'s. She says, 'I thought bodies were designed to heal themselves.'

He stares at her. Lets the room fill with silence. Points to the images on his screen, then asks, 'How much of your life does this affect?'

'Everything,' she says.

'Everything,' he repeats. 'Work? Driving? Dressing? Sleep?'

She nods.

'Leisure? All of the things you like to do?'

She nods.

'Relationships? Sex?'

She stares at him.

He holds up the hardware in front of her, as if she has not seen it for what it is. 'This,' he says, 'is *designed*. Bodies are not.' He looks at her. Smiles. 'If bodies healed themselves I'd be out of a job, wouldn't I?'

She takes the prosthesis back into her hands. She traces her fingers over its cool, intricate surfaces. In a way, it's a beautiful thing to build into one's self. Amazing. Amazing. Amazing.

She looks around the room once more, avoiding his face because she knows she is about to cry. She recognises, vaguely, that the pens and the mouse pad and the notebooks on his desk each bear the same brand name as that inscribed on the object in her hand.

He plucks the prosthesis back from her. He turns it slowly in the light, admiring it. 'Look,' he says, 'if you don't do this, you will end up crippled. You will be in pain for the rest of your life.'

Her face rushes red. Tears threaten. She can't tell whether it's fury or fear storming the salt and the blood inside her.

He gets up. Shakes her hand. Dismisses her.

By the time she gets home a slow panic pulses through her. She googles the neurosurgeon's name. He has his own website. His face grins out from the homepage: a car salesman in mint-coloured scrubs. His services are listed down one side of the screen: craniotomy, lobectomy, discectomy, laminectomy, vertebrectomy, discography, fusion, corpectomy. The list goes on and on. She clicks on 'Complications': infection, bleeding, paralysis, stroke, DVT, death. She finds a link to 'Hobbies': kids and dogs and tennis; footy and violin; Christianity. She stares, but she cannot assess what she is looking at.

A Christian man?

A belief in God?

A belief he's God?

She has no idea, now, what to make of anything.

Ø

This is her first time in the gym. She is waiting for a personal trainer to come and give her some advice.

She stands in a corner, self-conscious in tight black pants. Across the room a huge poster hangs from the ceiling, shivering in the draught from the air conditioner. On it, a petite bronzed girl beats gloved fists into a boxing bag. Beneath her, in a fire of red letters: 'Empower Yourself!'

The gym walls are made of glass. On one side, the glass is fogged from the swimming pool. The remaining walls face the car park, the street, and the refinery. Dozens of treadmills are lined up in rows, staring at the sunburnt, steel-gripped horizon.

Though the room is huge, it seems to be full of people, all of them running, running, running. No-one looks outside. Instead, everyone looks up at the silent televisions suspended from the ceiling. Teletext streams across the screens. Dance music palpitates, cutting through everything. A hard white light blasts in from the street, detailing every blotch and line and flinch in people's faces. Sheens of sweat shine from every stretch of flesh, and there is nothing to soften the savage thuds of each body's jerk and jolt, weight colliding again and again into steel and rubber.

A fat man walks on a machine near the end of a row of treadmills. He stares up at the televisions. A painful V of sweat creeps down his front and back. Once in a while his feet trip over themselves, confused by the false earth moving beneath them. Most of the treadmills are occupied, except for those closest to him. He is a horror of obesity.

The instructor is late, so she waits, focusing on the good-looking couple at the far side of the room. They run next to each other on the treadmills, pushing themselves harder and harder and *harder*. The more she stares the more they look like automatons: strange machines upon strange machines. Watching them, that old feeling creeps up her throat. The choking terror of the archetypal nightmare: hunted, running, but getting nowhere.

The fat man presses a button on his treadmill and begins to jog. He stares down at his feet. The fingertips of one hand rest on the side rail, steadying him. His other arm beats time at his side, the fat flapping like the plucked wing of an enormous turkey.

Someone taps her on the shoulder. It's the trainer. He looks about eighteen. She stares at the boils blistering across the white, clammy skin of his neck. His cheeks are scarlet, his forehead dripping.

He smiles, and apologises, but will not meet her eye. Instead, he stares out at the heat-haze of the refinery, and begins to describe his personalised fitness program.

She nods, but then she is turning, walking away, and leaving his voice behind her.

Ten minutes later she is swimming across the blue, the only sound in her ears, her breathing.

Ø

She borrows more money and pays to see two more specialists. They are both angered by Green Eyes' advice, and by his quote for the surgery he says she must have. They both tell her to ignore him, and to wait and see if she gets better on her own. Bodies heal themselves, they say, most of the time. They are too busy to answer her questions. They give her some pamphlets telling her how to get better. One pamphlet recommends that she do exactly what the other warns her not to.

She goes to the public hospital and asks when she'll be able to discuss her scan with one of the surgeons. The receptionist shrugs: a letter will come in the mail.

She goes to a physio.

'That's *bad*,' the young woman says, looking up from the scan. 'That's the worst I've *ever* seen.' She recommends an eight-week course of one-on-one Pilates. She whips out a white snake of spine to explain the problem's physiology. 'You must reactivate your *transversus abdominis*.' She stands and lifts her top. She points to her stomach. 'It's like a girdle, yeah? Look, I'm clenching it ... *now*.' The expression drops from her face. A quiver moves across her tight, flat stomach. 'See?' She sits down again. 'You've gotta get onto this right away, before they *butcher* you up.' The physio throws the naked spine across the room, where it hits the wall and clatters into a basket of body parts.

She goes to a chiro, who stands her up, lies her down, and tells her it's really her hips that are the problem. 'They're misaligned,' he says, 'so all of you is misaligned, top to toe. Cause and effect. You need realigning,' he says, nodding to himself. He pats her hand. 'Don't worry,' he says. He recommends two appointments per week.

She goes back to her GP. He also tells her to ignore Green Eyes. She asks lots of questions about worst-case scenarios. He tells her to keep away from Google. He shrugs his shoulders about the gym, the physio, the chiro, the neuros. 'No-one really knows,' he says. 'Just take it easy, listen to your body, wait and see.'

'For how long?'

Again, he shrugs. 'Till it's a lot better, or a lot worse.' He stares at her flushed face.

'I can't tell anymore,' she says, 'what's pain and what's fear.'

He has known her since she was two blue lines on a pee-wetted stick. 'Don't worry,' he says, looking worried. He reaches for his prescription pad.

Though he's just told her to listen to her body, he offers her the one thing he can. Chemical gags. Painkillers. Lots of them. Whatever she wants.

Alone at home, not sure what to do—and therefore doing nothing—the internet lures her in: she is googling for a solution, reassurance. She finds horror stories, as she knew she would. She finds testimonies for and against every product, exercise, medical discipline. Everywhere, threats and promises. Everywhere, despair and hopelessness. Everywhere, digital screams into the ether.

Ø

She swims. The novelty has worn off. She resents how her skin and hair have dried up, how she always smells like chlorine. She's been swimming for months, but still she struggles for breath. Perhaps, she thinks, it's an anxiety thing, a reaction to the communality of the water, to the webs of phlegm floating by like strange, self-annihilating jellyfish. Hair, stained Band-Aids, snow-motes of skin. She is ingesting what the others leave behind.

One day, as she nears the end of her lane, she sees the bruised, ulcerated legs of an old, old man. Gnarled red corals, they plant him to the floor of the pool. Slowly, painfully, he raises and lowers himself on his toes. Through the water-light, she watches the delicate scales of skin flap gently up and down in time with his movement. We are all beautiful, she thinks. We are all beautiful. She watches one of the scales dislodge and drift towards her, propelled by the ripples of his movement, resisting the ripple of hers.

She stands, smiles at the man.

He winks at her. 'Use it or lose it, eh, love?' He openly admires her breasts, stomach, thighs.

In the change room, she presses the shower's timed button again and again.

Ø

The day of her public hospital appointment finally comes. She does not know if the man speaking to her is an intern, registrar or surgeon. He could be a cleaner, for all she knows. Though she has spent eight months waiting and seeing, he flicks through her scans and tells her she must wait and see.

Afterwards, she wanders the hospital looking for a way out. Finds herself in intensive care. She panics as the images imprint: a face sunk into plaster (trapped, trapped); a woman wired into the walls (amazing, amazing); dark stains on a stretch of white (as intimate as sex, as intimate as sex).

In the hospital cafeteria, she tries to calm down.

A teenage boy sits near her. Pieces of fabric and plastic and foam are strapped across his head, snug, like a wrestler's helmet. An older couple joins him. As they organise themselves, the boy carefully unbuckles his helmet and dumps it on the table. Silver rivers lace through the intricate topography of lumps and bumps that undulate across his scalp. He scratches at the scrubs of hair that have begun to grow in the shorn softness between the scars.

He chugs down his soft drink, all at once. He burps.

His mother looks up sharply, but his giggling gets her laughing too. She makes to slap him.

'Not the head!' he laughs. 'Not the head!'

People turn to look. Quickly, they look away.

The boy fiddles with his helmet, his eyes wandering the cafeteria. For a second, his gaze meets hers. From him, half a smile, half a shrug. He begins to flush. He looks back down at the table. He can't be older than sixteen, barely half her age.

She gathers her things, turns and walks out into the sunstruck autumn day.

Ø

Winter again. Long, dark mornings. She rests at the end of a lap, looking out at the fog-blurred lights of the refinery. It's a terrible beauty. How she loves it.

She breathes more easily now. The webs of hair, the ghosts of spit and the spawn-clouds of shed skin no longer bother her. Head under, watching, she lets it all pass by and through her. None of it has harmed her yet.

The limp-handed man overtakes her. He is a better swimmer than she'll ever be. She watches his hands, one good, one bad, as they arc through the water with equal grace, both of them pulling him along. Beautiful. He moves on ahead, in front of her. She swims in his wake. In this tunnel of bubbles that he has given her, the resistance of the water seems to disappear altogether.

She is weightless.

Nothing, she thinks, no-one, will ever make us sink.

MORNING SONG

THE WOMAN WHO stands on the doorstep is short and chunky. Her legs are like an elephant's. They go up from her feet and down from her hips without contour or curve. Her hair is coloured a bright red. Henna hair. Curly. Messy. Already, curls are plastered to her sticky pink cheeks. Already, there are lines of sweat where her vest has been trapped between the tumbles and turns of her stomach.

The woman who answers the door is very tall and very thin. She is wearing a suit: grey, tailored, costly. Her fair hair has been carefully coloured and blow-waved. Her face is made up in soft pastel shades. She wears amber in her ears and a matching pendant hangs around her neck, huge and heavy and cool. She could be thirty. She could be forty.

The women embrace.

Ø

Inside, the chunky woman waits for her friend to get ready. She stands in the kitchen and looks out through the vast wall of windows to the blazing garden. Though this is the eighth and worst year of the drought, everything looks lush and green, and the leaves of the gums flash and glitter as though they have been washed with rain. The chunky woman stares at the perfectly manicured grass. It glitters too. From somewhere high up above the house, a magpie's song sets the heat shimmering.

The thin woman comes into the kitchen. She turns in a mock pirouette. 'How do I look?' She smiles. She laughs, then she is fanning her eyes with one of her hands. 'Oh God,' she laughs. 'Sorry,' she laughs. Her tears brim, but do not fall, not even when her voice stumbles as she looks down at the chunky woman's worried face and says, 'Is it too soon? Is it?'

The chunky woman takes her friend's shaking hands and squeezes them and kisses them.

Again, the magpie yodels.

'Be careful,' the thin woman says, pulling her hands free. 'There's a nest,' she says, pointing to the ceiling, 'and they're swooping.' She smiles again and jerks her narrow shoulders back theatrically. She stands tall and nods. She gathers her things and gathers herself and makes to leave. Suddenly, she half turns and awkwardly kisses the chunky woman full on the lips. 'Thanks,' she says, as the chunky woman laughs and pushes her away and slaps her backside and wipes her mouth with mock disgust.

The thin woman hurries down the hall and out into the scorching street.

The chunky woman bends and presses her damp, flushed face against the cool marble counter.

Ø

The chunky woman sits on a chair next to the baby's cot. The radio plays from the kitchen. There is an empty coffee cup on the floor next to her foot.

She looks at the baby. He is asleep. His fat arms are thrown above his head, fists clenched. His eyes scrunch up occasionally, as if his dreams worry him.

The chunky woman looks out the window. The magpie sits on the fence, staring in. She is big. Her slick feathers flash back the glare. Her face is satiny soft, her beak chalky white except for its oil-black, dagger-sharp tip. She hops left. She hops right. She cocks a reddish eye at the window. Hops left, hops right. She is looking at something, looking for something. Perhaps she is just looking at her reflection.

'Looking for baby, birdy?' the chunky woman asks, standing. The bird drops from the fence, then swoops up and away, out of sight.

The chunky woman leans over the cot. The baby's skin looks mottled, pink and blue. She runs one finger up his arm. She pulls her hand back. Stares. The baby is very still. She makes a coughing sound. His chest does not move. His eyelids do not flicker. Perhaps a few seconds pass, perhaps thirty, perhaps a minute.

The chunky woman lunges over the edge of the cot. She is shaking the baby's tummy. Shaking the whole baby with her hand on his tummy. 'Breathe,' she says, her voice cracking. '*Breathe*, you bastard!'

The baby's face suddenly contorts. He arches his back, splutters, and gulps in a big, grumbling breath. His arms spasm above his head, then return to their luxurious reclined pose. Slowly, his fists unclench. He breathes regularly again.

The chunky woman stands over the baby, watching. She places the tip of her finger in his palm. Anemone-like, his fingers close around hers. His grip is strong. Carefully, she disentangles herself and steps away from the cot.

The chunky woman wanders around the room, picking things up, putting them down. There are soft toys in a box under the window. There are piles of tiny, neatly ironed clothes and a mountain of disposable nappies on a chest of drawers. Against the back wall, lined up on the white-painted shelves, are dozens of books. She runs her finger along the titles. Lots of famous names. She selects a book randomly and takes it back to her chair.

She flicks through it, stopping at a double-page colour image. It shows a naked woman on all fours in an inflatable paddling pool. She wears a sweatband and her hair is pulled up in a high ponytail. A man kneels next to her in the water. He is also naked. A long, curly mullet frames his cheesy grin as he cheers her on. A mucousy, bloody baby's head is emerging from between the woman's buttocks. 'Jesus,' the chunky woman mutters, slamming the book shut. 'Jesus *Christ*.' She tosses it to the floor where it lands with a loud slap.

The baby mumbles.

After a moment, the chunky woman stands, picks up the book, dusts it off and returns it to the shelf. She wanders back to the cot.

The baby's face ripples. His eyes flash open. He begins to holler.

The chunky woman stands over him, watching. 'Wah wah wah,' she says, staring down at his wrinkly red face. The baby's arms punch about. His legs kick the flannelette blanket so that his naked, arching belly is uncovered.

She looks out the window.

The baby keeps crying. Not louder and louder, not softer and softer, just a steady monotone yelling.

Eventually, she reaches into the cot and jerks the sheet right down. 'You stink,' she says, inspecting the mattress and the covers. 'You *stink*.' She picks him up and carries him at arm's length to the plastic-sheeted change table.

She lays him down and opens his nappy. He and the nappy are covered in a greenish-yellow sludge. She turns her head away as much as she can. She lifts the baby's legs with one hand and extracts the nappy with the other. Quickly, she folds the mess away, sealing it up tightly in a plastic bag. She grabs a handful of wet wipes and cleans the mess from the baby's body and the plastic sheeting. She packs the filthy wipes into another plastic bag.

'Deeee-sgusting!' the chunky woman says, smiling down at his clean body. Wide-eyed, he smiles back. 'Dee-dee-deeeeee-sgusting,' she sings. He laughs. He looks up at her. He blinks, blinks, and then looks over her head. She follows his gaze. A ribbon of colourful beads suspends a glass prism from the light fitting. The crystal turns slowly on its axis, catching the light and moving rainbows across the walls.

She looks back down at the baby. His face is no longer an ugly red. His eyes are a pale, staring blue. His forehead is large and bulbous. The chunky woman traces the line that marks where the left and right parts of his brain meet. She touches the wide crater of his belly button. She presses into it. He does not seem to mind. She studies his perfectly formed fingers and toes and each of his tiny, translucent nails. She looks at his smooth, firm nostrils. The sheen of skin on his eyelids. His almost invisible lashes and brows. His thin, pink, wet lips. His mouth opens. He grizzles, revealing bone-hard gums. She looks at the loose skin between his legs. She gently pokes it with her finger, watching the skin flop about as he joyfully kicks his feet.

The baby doesn't register her disgust. Instead, he laughs again, his hands reaching for her face.

She gets a fresh nappy. Returns to the change table. The baby has become very quiet and very still. The chunky woman hesitates, watching. Then his penis stiffens and a neat arc of urine sprays the chunky woman in the face and across her front. She stands there, silent and dripping. Stares down at his squirming form. He kicks his legs and pumps his arms, chuckling.

Ø

The baby has been fed and tucked into his cot. With the monitor in tow, the chunky woman leaves him and wanders around the thin woman's house.

Everything is spotless: all whiteness and windows, slate and steel. Everything, except the snatches of colour that catch her eye and draw her through the rooms. Here, a gaudy handmade cushion on the cream leather couch. There, a blue plastic picture frame cast in the shape of a rabbit; mother, father and baby smile from a circle cut out of its belly. Here, a mess of knitting shoved under a glass-topped coffee table. There, on the floor, behind the big-screen TV, two bright yellow gaming consoles nestled in a tangle of cords.

Now and again the chunky woman puts the monitor to her ear. Baby mumbles to himself. He giggles and jabbers and gripes. She wanders on. Finds the main bedroom. Stops in the doorway: no glass and slate and steel in here. Instead, wood. A big jarrah bed faces the window. Matching sets of drawers sit on either side, each adorned with a small leadlight lamp. An antique wardrobe rests against the far wall. The velvet curtains that frame the sash window are the same deep red as the blanket draped across the bed.

The chunky woman sits down. She props the monitor under one of the lamps. She lifts the blanket up. She buries her face in the red wool as the baby's chatter slowly fills the room.

Eventually, she puts the blanket down. She reads the spines of the books stacked under the lamp. Sees blood-blotched tissues rumpled next to them. Sees a ring, a pair of earrings, and an envelope. The chunky woman pulls a letter from the envelope and reads it. Pulls out photos and studies them. Carefully returns everything to its place. She leans forward and opens the top drawer. She finds more envelopes in here. More letters posted from the same country as the other. More photos of the thin woman's parents. She finds some souvenirs from overseas: key rings, postcards, a cigarette lighter in the shape of a naked woman with 'Paris' emblazoned across her breasts. The chunky woman flicks the lighter on: the figure's head rears back and a flame bursts out of her cleaved neck. There are more photos tucked into the back of the drawer, folded between sheets of fine yellow paper.

These photos are different. They're older. These are photos of the thin woman as a baby, as a toddler, as a girl. These are photos of the thin woman and the chunky woman as teenagers, as twenty-somethings. In one they are all wrapped up in each other on a picnic rug, their tightly jeaned legs entwined, their bright shirts twisted and rolled up to reveal tanned arms and stomachs. They are kissing and laughing. There's a photo of the thin woman's husband sunning himself next to a scabby heeler on someone's veranda. There's a photo of him naked, running into the surf. There's a photo of him asleep with his arms thrown over his head, just as the baby's were this morning. There are photos of other men too; men the chunky woman does not recognise.

One photo pulls her up short. She puts the other photos down on the bed, and brings this picture close to her face. There is the baby, filling up most of the frame. He is naked. His head is conical, squashed. His forehead and shoulders are covered in black fuzz. Everything is slicked with blood and gunk. There is a clip on his fat purple umbilical cord. If it weren't for his scream-torn face, he'd look dead. The thin woman is in the background, looking past the baby at the photographer. Though she is slightly out of focus, the chunky woman can see the tears streaming down her bloated red cheeks. She looks exhausted.

The chunky woman sits up straight, the photo resting in her lap. With one shaking hand, she neatly flicks the tears from her eyes, flick-flick, flick-flick. She picks up a bloodied tissue from the chest of drawers and carefully dabs her face. She sniffs sharply, replaces the tissue, and sets about jumbling the photographs back into order. She returns them to the drawer.

Ø

Late in the afternoon, the chunky woman takes the disgruntled baby into the yard. The day's heat is finally subsiding. Only now does she realise that the lush manicured lawn is made from plastic.

'What do you want?' she asks, holding the baby in one arm whilst spreading a blanket on the turf with the other. The baby squirms in her clutch. He huffs and puffs, murmurs and wriggles. She looks down at him. His face creases and he lets out a sorrowful yowl.

She laughs. She carefully lays him on his stomach. He stops crying. She watches as he tries to lift himself up. His head remains face down, flat on the blanket. His hands open and close, clutching at the rough wool.

'Stupid,' she says, gently turning him on his back. 'Stupid baby.'

She lies next to him. They stare up at one of the biggest gum trees. The deep peachy-pink of its trunk and branches glows in the light of the dying sun. The bark stretches up the tree's length, smooth as skin, gathering into gentle folds around each amputation and knot and explosion of sap.

The baby begins to settle. Together, they watch the long thin silhouettes of the leaves move above them. Blotches of light dance over their faces and warm their skin. The baby's hands chase the shadows, or the light, or the leaves, or the sky, or the breeze as it conducts a dry symphony around them.

'Look,' the chunky woman says, pointing upwards.

The baby kicks his legs about. Ignores her.

The magpie perches on one of the gum's knotted, pink arms. She hops, looks down, hops, leans over to get a better look at them and almost topples off the branch.

The chunky woman laughs.

The magpie scrambles about, rights herself and stares down again, her dark eyes twitching.

Then, she swoops.

As the bird drops towards them, the chunky woman reaches one arm out and over the baby, covering his face. Her free hand presses firmly towards the bird, like that of a policeman directing traffic to a stop. The magpie understands. She glides silently across them and over to the neighbour's almond tree. There, she turns, hops, cocks her head and continues to watch them.

The chunky woman rolls over and raises herself on her elbows, positioning her chest and arms over the baby so he is hidden from the magpie's view.

The baby begins to grizzle.

'Don't cry,' the chunky woman growls. '*Don't!*'

The baby hesitates. One of his hands flings out and smacks her chin. He laughs. Kicks his legs.

'*Bad* baby!' she says, her voice angry. She thumps her hands down on either side of his head. The plastic grass crackles.

The baby's whole body freezes. He stares. His wet lips tremble.

'You know what happens to bad, bad bay-bees?' she sings.

The baby smiles and spits and laughs and kicks her breasts with his soft bare feet.

She pinches and prods him and clicks her fingers about his head.

He laughs. He frowns. He hovers on tears.

She darts a pointed finger back and forth from one of his eyes. He blinks. His hands grab at her.

'Good bay-bee,' she sings.

Eventually, the chunky woman rolls away. She lies on her back and looks for the magpie. The bird is gone.

She looks over again at the baby. The blotches of light have resumed their dance across his pale, wriggling form. She rests a hand on his stomach, watches the shadows move from his skin, to hers, and back again. She taps out a rhythm with the flats of her fingers, as if his belly is a drum. He ignores her.

She props herself up on her elbows and surveys the garden again. It is empty. She gets up and goes inside.

Ø

She can see the baby from where she works. Heavy and slow, she prepares another bottle of the thin woman's milk.

She returns with the bottle. She stands over the baby and looks down. He stares up at her. She clucks her tongue. She kneels next to him. He laughs and slaps at the air and jiggles his feet. Carefully, she picks him up. Carefully, she crooks him in her arm.

She begins to rock him. She sucks the rubber nipple, warming it, wetting it. Then she rubs it across the baby's lips. His mouth opens, slimy and red and reaching. The chunky woman stops rocking. Pulls the bottle away. Slowly, she stretches down the low-cut neck of her own top. She takes one of her breasts out of her bra. Immediately, he reaches for it. She winces as his hard gums clamp down on her nipple. His hands clutch and knead at her breast. His face draws in on itself as he begins to suck.

For a while she just sits there, like that, staring down at the baby's hot mouth clamped on her nipple.

Soon, the baby begins to grumble. Suddenly he withdraws and hits her breast away. He starts to wail.

The chunky woman watches him. Again, she takes the bottle and sucks the rubber nipple. Again, she rubs it against the baby's lips. He stops crying and latches onto it. His hands come up and grip her fingers. As he sucks she puts her breast back into her bra and rearranges her top.

The baby concentrates, sucking and sucking and sucking. The chunky woman looks away, and begins to count the plastic blades of grass, glowing in the warming light of the last sun. Finally, he is asleep.

The back door slides open. The chunky woman looks up. With a smooth, dull thud the door rolls shut again. The thin woman stands there, her bag in one hand, staring.

The two women's eyes meet.

'How'd it go?' the chunky woman asks.

The thin woman nods her head slightly, says nothing.

Around them, the night-song of the crickets begins to pulse.

From where she kneels, the chunky woman holds the baby up, offering him back to his mother.

Her friend walks over. She puts down her bag. Picks him up. Cuddles him close.

The chunky woman rocks back on her heels, ready to rise, but stumbles in surprise.

A flashing blur of black and white.

A soft, dry beat.

The magpie swoops between them, then flies up into the gum tips.

The chunky woman stands and stares into the blackening leaves. She cannot see the bird, but as she turns to the thin woman its song suddenly uncurls into the dusk, ringing out like a call to prayer.

The chunky woman smiles and looks at her friend.

The thin woman pays no attention. She is wandering in circles around the garden, rocking her baby and singing to him in her soft and tuneless voice.

ADRIAN

For each man kills the thing he loves,
Yet each man does not die.
Oscar Wilde

EVERYBODY KNOWS THAT if you meet your doppel-gänger, that shadow self who goes about the world clothed in your image, then either one or both of you will die. As the second-born son, Adrian must have had a lesser claim on the world than his elder brother—my father—for it was he who died first.

Ø

'Dad, why didn't you tell me you had a pet cockatoo?'
My father stared at me and then jerked the photo out

of my hands. Towering above me, he stared blankly at the picture and said nothing. 'Well? Why didn't you tell me you had a pet cockatoo?' At eight years of age, animals were my sole preoccupation. All of my time was spent caring for bottled insects, caged guinea pigs and tanked goldfish. I can't remember how I found that photograph, but I do remember the sense of betrayal that surged through me as I studied it: Why hadn't my dad told me he'd once owned a parrot? In response to my question—which had become a demand—my dad looked down at me. Still, he said nothing. Unable to interpret his mixed-up look or his muteness, and sensing trouble, I scuttled away. I left him there on the cool cork tiles, stunned and silent, with that glassed-in mirror image of himself held tightly in his hands.

Ø

Here is the photo from that day. It shows a man with a cockatoo perched on his tanned forearm. You can tell that the man loves the bird: his body is turned towards it, excluding everything else. There is a smile around his eyes and the bird looks up at him fearlessly. They look like they are deep in conversation. This man in the photo is identical to my dad. He has the same big nose, with the bump in the middle. The same brown skin. The same chin and jaw and cheeks. He even has the same black hair, parted and brushed to one side, in just the same style. This man in the photo is identical to my father, but he is not my father. He is Adrian, my father's younger brother, a man I never knew.

Ø

By the time I was thirteen I had proven to my parents that I was 'a responsible young woman'. Over the years, I'd cared for Rex the guinea pig, Hermie the hermit crab, and Goldie the goldfish. I was ready for something more challenging, something with which I could have a more intimate relationship. Whilst a boyfriend would have been the obvious choice, my parents were no doubt relieved when I became fixated on parrots. I spent hours reading about their different types, how to feed and house them, and—most importantly of all—how to make them talk. I terrified myself with stories of macaws and other exotic species that had gouged out eyes, or ripped noses off unsuspecting faces. Everything I read about these birds frightened me, but I pushed this fear aside with a growing determination that a parrot would be—must be—mine.

Ø

Adrian's story always begins with its end. His death. Leukaemia. That long, prickly word that I am learning to write but still cannot say. The word that killed Lorraine, their sister, when she was seven years old. The word that, like his nose and chin and jaw, links Adrian to my dad—whose own blood has just begun its battle against that word's too-concrete implications.

'How did you find out Adrian was sick?'

We are sitting in a café. Fool enough to think the past has passed, I am asking my father about his brother.

'I don't know.' He fidgets. 'I can't remember. There were four of you kids by then. And there was work.' He shakes his head. 'I can't remember.'

'Does it make you feel guilty?'

'What?'

'That you will be okay?'

Unlike Adrian, my dad has been lucky: time and science have found a way to convince his blood and bone that they are well.

'No.' He shakes his head again. 'I don't feel guilty.'

Sensing his embarrassment, I divert our talk down another path of the story. 'Did he meet Grace before or after he was diagnosed?'

'After.'

'So she married him knowing what was going to happen?'

He nods.

Ø

In the end, I decided that a cockatoo was the right bird to get. My diary from that time shows how my research into the science of taming parrots ultimately forced my choice. Notes and sketches are scrawled all over the diary's pink pages, each of them copied carefully from library books and my imagination. These notes conclude with a list of the pros and cons attached to my two favoured birds: 'Macaw beautiful and smart; Cocky plainer and dumber. Macaw will rip off face; Cocky probably won't. Macaw expensive; Cocky cheap and Aussie'. In this diary I can find no evidence that Adrian's photo influenced my choice. My thirteen-year-old memory seems to have forgotten my encounter with the photograph some five years before. Nowhere on the diary's pages have I written, 'Dad had a cockatoo too'.

Ø

This woman, Grace. Without her, I think Adrian's image would disappear under the weight of that too-encompassing word 'tragedy'. Just another tragedy. Grace and Adrian's love—if that is what they called it—must have been such a mess of ambivalence, yet when I think of her I see her pulling that mess down around them like a blanket, tucking them into a private world of intimacies that no-one was allowed to spectate or judge or intrude upon.

The one picture I found of Grace is disappointing. She wears her wedding dress. She looks plain. Ordinary. She does not look like the kind of woman who is marrying a man knowing that he will die and that he will die badly.

'He was diagnosed, but he seemed so well.' Again, my dad fidgets. I want to grab his hand and press it firmly to the table. Instead, my silence forces him to struggle on. 'He looked normal. Healthy. They must have hoped he'd recover. Then it happened, all at once, as it does. And that was it.'

His blunt and bitten finger follows the patterns in the laminate tabletop. I watch his tracings. Avoid his face.

He stops fidgeting and looks up at me. 'I feel guilty when I think of his life. Of how he saw his life. Of how my father saw him. Or didn't see him. How we never talked about anything that mattered.' He looks down again. Begins retracing the tabletop. 'Adrian never *said* anything about all that. But somehow we both knew that I was the golden boy. I could do no wrong. He could do no right. He thought I had everything. The education, the job, the wife, the children … Everything he didn't have, until the end, when he had Grace.'

'When it was too late,' I say, immediately regretting the stupid obviousness of my words. I quickly ask another question. 'Do you remember the wedding?'

He shakes his head, still staring at the table. 'I told you,' he says, 'I don't remember anything. I never *knew* anything to remember. That's the worst thing—not the forgetting, but the never knowing.'

Ø

When I had decided upon a cockatoo, my dad and I set about converting our old tree house into an aviary. We thought the bird would appreciate being up there in the apple tree, gazing out the windows into the leaves and the branches and the endless blue sky. We spent days sawing and sanding and painting, both of us certain that our cockatoo would be as impressed with its new airborne home as we were.

Once the aviary was finished, we drove to a big outer-suburban pet shop that specialised in parrots. When we walked inside, the first bird we spotted was a macaw. It sat, proud and huge in its blue and yellow plumage, at the very centre of the room. A price tag for thousands was tied to its stand. Recalling stories of bloody eye sockets and torn flesh, I tried to ignore the bird's haughty gaze as we nervously looked for 'our' cockatoo. Soon enough, we found one that met my criteria for selection: young (easier to tame), and energetic (not diseased). As we left the store, carrying the bird in a shoebox, the owner assured us we'd have no trouble.

'No trouble at all!' the macaw screeched. 'No trouble at all!'

The owner turned, furious, and yelled at it to *shut up*.

'Shut up!' the macaw repeated, in perfect imitation. 'Shut up!' Then it laughed and laughed. Its cackle followed us out of the shop and echoed between us on our silent, nervous drive home.

Ø

I realise that I am not asking my dad about Adrian. I am asking, instead, for a story. But a person is not a story. A person is a half-known chaos of impressions, and that is all that my dad can give me.

'Who was there in the end?' In the end. How hard

it is to find the words with which to ask these questions.

He sighs and sits back in his chair. He looks tired. 'We were all there—coming and going—but I mostly remember the times I was alone with him. And I remember him asking me to sit him up. He knew there wasn't long, and he wanted to be sat up.'

Suddenly I don't want to know anymore. I can sense the crudeness of this conversation. My voyeurism. My intrusion into an old privacy that does not belong to me.

My dad pushes his empty coffee cup away. 'Do you know what Adrian asked me, near the end?'

I shake my head. I want to say, 'Stop! It's not for me or anyone else to know.' Instead, I remain silent.

'He asked me if his life had been a complete waste.' My dad looks at me. 'And do you know what I said? Nothing. I said *nothing*.'

Ø

For weeks I spent hours each day, before and after school, sitting in the tree house trying to tame Peppie. Each day I sat there terrified as the tormented creature spread his wings to their full three-foot span, lifted his lemon-yellow crest and lunged at me, and again lunged at me. He only stopped doing this when I brought him almonds. Then, he would shift from foot to foot, size me up against my offer of sweets, suddenly grab the nut from my fingers, and hop it over to the other side of his perch. There, he'd hold the nut in his clawed foot and chew it whilst appraising me with a cool, cocked eye. I knew that too many nuts were bad for him, but I brought them anyway in the vain and hardly admitted hope that I could buy his affection.

It quickly became clear that my almond bribes were not working. Peppie still raised his crest, lifted his wings, and lunged at me. My thirteen-year-old feelings were crushed by his behaviour. I became withdrawn, mute with shame and embarrassment and a pride that refused to admit to my smirking brothers or my worried parents that I had been wrong. I realised what a sick form of torture we'd made for that bird, casting its home high up in a sky that it could not fly in. I realised that the problem was not that Peppie was *going* wild, but that he had always been wild. He was meant to be wild.

Ø

'So you were there when he died?'

My father nods. The waitress comes over and takes our cups, asking us if we'd like another. He smiles at her, shakes his head.

'And Granny was there?'

Again, he nods. 'When it finally happened, your granny was there. She was there with us.'

'Did she say anything? Did he say anything to her?'

'No. He just died. And it was quiet. Your granny stood at the end of the bed. She didn't move, had no expression. She'd always said that after losing Lorraine, she'd never cry again.'

Ø

One morning, going out to do my time with the hated and hating bird, I found that he had disappeared. Excited and afraid, I ran around the apple tree and spotted him sitting in its branches. He looked slyly down at me. I ran back into the house. 'Mum! Dad! Peppie's in the garden!'

My father mumbled something about how, earlier that morning, he'd cut a hole in the aviary's wire so that Peppie could 'hop in and out as he pleased'. My parents assured me that *of course* everything would be all right— despite the bird's clipped and flightless wings—and that *of course* Peppie would still be our pet and would become tame and would join us, one day, in the house.

Later, home from school, I raced to the tree house to see if Peppie was okay. But he wasn't there. He wasn't in the branches of the apple tree or the gum tree or the almond tree—the one tree I was sure would keep him close to us forever.

As I turned back to the house, a high-pitched squawking suddenly sounded over the back fence. I ran towards it and listened, seeing with my ears everything that was happening in our neighbours' yard.

A growling replied to the squawking.

A door creaked open and slammed shut.

A snarl. A high-pitched yelp.

A person shouting, 'Hell! A bloody *bird's* bitten off his *nose!*'

A low whining grumble—a nightmare sound, heavy with pain and warning.

Silence, and I remember seeing, in my mind, the

bloody-faced dog circling my Peppie, circling the silence and then tensing itself low to the ground.

A shriek. A piercing squawk.

Then, there was nothing.

I knew that Peppie was dead. I knew that I had killed him.

Ø

'What happened to his bird?'

'What bird?'

'Adrian's cockatoo, the one in the photo.'

My dad smiles, remembering the photograph. When I rediscovered it last year I presented it to him just as I had twenty years before. He recognised my gesture. Remembered my angry eight-year-old face demanding answers about his mysterious past as an owner of exotic pets. He told me of his shock at my childish certainty that the photo was of him. For a moment, he said, he'd felt like he'd become his brother's ghost.

My father's smile doesn't last, and he almost sounds angry when he says, 'He loved that bird! He'd had it forever. He found it when it was a chick, tamed it ... I think he thought that bird was his great success. He didn't trust any of us to understand. Didn't think we would care for her as he had.'

I stare at my dad's hands, splayed on the table. I remember his excitement as we spent days in the apple tree, building that aviary. I remember his sadness as he watched it all fall apart, how he too fought back tears as

I fled from Peppie's mauling.

I stare at my dad's hands, and listen to him end his brother's story. 'When Adrian realised he was dying—that he wouldn't get better—he took the bird out into his garden, and broke her neck.'

How strange that Adrian's life ended with leukaemia, whilst his story ends—and can only end—with the death of his bird.

'How do you know he did that?'

My father shrugs his shoulders. 'I don't know.' He shakes his head. 'I don't know how I know that. I wasn't there. But every time I think of Adrian that is what I see. I don't see him dying, or asking me about his wasted life. I don't see any of the things I actually saw. I just see him holding that bird and talking to her for the last time—as if everything was normal—then wringing her neck.'

Ø

I don't ask my father about Peppie. We just sit here quietly. Again, I see us up in an apple tree, trying to make real two linked, but different, daydreams. I see my dad creeping out, one morning, to cut a hole in the cage that he had built. He was fixing the one thing that he could—my distress—but in doing so he was accepting the immutability of what had long ago passed: Adrian, over twenty years dead, the second-born son, the identical other for whom the world was too small.

WHAT THERE IS

EVERY NIGHT, SHE sits at the front of our café. She faces the street. She crosses her left leg over her right, rests her elbow on the table, places her cheek in the palm of her raised hand, and stares out at the ocean. Behind the counter, I pretend to clean glass surfaces whilst watching her watch a day's worth of traffic going home.

Mark won't look at her. Not anymore. He says, 'She's as bad as the others. You just like her because she's pretty.'

At first, we thought it important that we provided a place for people like her to come to. We thought our regulars came here to be seen—to be witnessed. It doesn't take long to remember a person's face, the seat they like to sit in, or the way they like their coffee made. It doesn't take long to work out if someone wants to talk or just be left alone.

We were entranced by the cool space that seemed to enclose each and every one of them. Mark said it was their histories orbiting around them like Saturn's icy rings, a floating sea of frozen tears. I thought it was their held-breath expanding them with anticipation as they waited at our café—*our* café—for their lives to begin.

She will glance to her left, away from the street and the sea. She will not look at me—never at Mark or at me—but over the counter. She will stare, for a second, at the mirrored tiles above the sink. She will see her thick, dark brows, her wide green eyes, her pale skin and her straight black hair. She will see her mouth too—closed, yet saying something with its shock of scarlet.

There is something in this act of looking for herself—of seeing herself—that seems to comfort her.

'Beauty is boring,' Mark says.

But hers is not, I do not say, and I cannot look away.

Ø

When I was twenty I'd take my brother, Ash, to a café in our street. We did this every day, clocking up hours together when I wasn't at work or uni. We normally sat in silence, but we didn't mind because there was no history of sex and hate and wrong decisions to destroy our silence with interpretation. And there was no future, either. We would say things if there were things to say, and say nothing if nothing was going. We tacked time down to the earth in the shape of this routine.

Then, one day, the silence changed. It pulled taut, made itself tangible. Ash tried to say something, stopped. Made to touch me, didn't. Finally, he sat back in his chair and mumbled, 'It's okay for *me*, all of this.' He turned his hands up so that they held the café. 'My life is ending,' he said, 'but you need to go, or you'll end up with nothing.'

We read. Mark reads quickly, scanning pages as if searching for evidence. 'Listen,' he says, and reads aloud details of a car crash, a war, a murder, a rape, a famine, a riot. Then he stares at me. I don't know what he wants. So I nod. He nods back, seeming satisfied that I have understood him and that we agree.

I read slowly, looking for something more obscure; something submerged in sentences, paragraphs, pages, and whole books. Word by word, I seek it: that body-jolt of recognition. For instance, I found this in the depths of a novel: 'happiness is repetition'. When I discovered that phrase, it was one of affirmation: repetition makes a promise of itself; repetition falls in love with itself; repetition threads minutes and hours and days together. That phrase made me understand my old ritual with Ash. Made it seem like something other than the compulsive, superstitious addiction I'd dismissed it for once he shoved me away. That phrase also explains all that happened after, for what did a café promise other than seven days of doing the same chores with the same people in the same place week in, week out, and forever? Repetition would be—must be—happiness. A wound demanded it. The past proved the method.

The formula seemed to work at first. Our new responsibilities structured our days and gave us a sense of purpose. We delighted in the simple magic of our routine. If tables were set up, people would come and sit in them. If food was prepared, people would come and eat it. If coffee was brewed, people would sniff their way through the door. Best of all was the promise that every day would begin and end with our shared solitude, sitting side by side in the front window, looking out to sea, talking about the day to come or the day just passed. 'An original life,' Mark used to say, pressing in close to me as he stared at the horizon. 'We've done it,' he'd say, glancing at me, then away again.

I didn't worry when our morning and evening talks diminished, then disappeared. It seemed only natural that the silence which characterised this broken edge of the world should begin to characterise us too. I told myself wordlessness was, as it had been with Ash, an expression of comfort and contentment. Books and poems assured me that silence was the best way to express the inexpressible: we were talking without talking; sharing by just being; understanding without saying.

Now I know better. Now I know that books and poems are just like people: dealers in hopes and half-truths.

Ø

Mark values each customer according to the number of hours they spend here. The less he sees them, the more he likes them. This is a reversal. At the beginning he, like me, developed affection for the people who kept returning to us. He would sit with the ones who could be sat with, and would nod at the ones who were unable to smile and unable to speak. 'They're in a rut,' he'd say, 'and they come here to get unstuck.' Now he hates the beautiful woman with the scarlet lips because she comes here every day. He smiles at strangers and avoids sitting with those whose name he knows. 'Leeches,' he calls them. 'Leeches and losers.'

The Professor is one of the regulars who has earned Mark's ire. He comes here for lunch at the same time every Thursday. He talks to himself. He makes a mess of his table, and sometimes he annoys other customers by chatting to them when they clearly want to be left alone. Over the years I've learned that his wife died decades ago, his daughters and grandchildren live overseas, and now he's being forced to retire from his job at the regional high school. The first thing he ever said to me was, 'Time, my dear, Time.' He looked at me for a moment. Sized something up. Concluded something else and proclaimed, 'Time!' He ordered a bowl of soup and a glass of our cheapest red wine. He has ordered that same meal, at the same time, on the same day, ever since.

When the café is quiet, I ask the Professor if I may sit with him. He tries to teach me about the possibilities of relativity and quantum theory and strings. He tries to make me understand that one day he will go back in time. 'It's only a matter of un-patterning the patterns,' he says, pulling a pen from a pocket and removing the napkin from under his bowl. He writes equations that bleed into the soft fibres of the tissue. He keeps looking at me to see if I am following him. I'm not, but I nod, so he continues filling his napkin with his science and his hope. I have boxes full of such things.

Mark barely tolerates the Professor. 'He's just a sad old kook,' he says, scrunching up a scribbled napkin before I have a chance to grab it. 'Just like the rest of them.'

Tonight—Tuesday night—the Professor surprises us by turning up for dinner. Mark flinches at the un-expected sight of him and disappears into the kitchen. The Professor smiles at me and moves to his table in the back corner of the café, slowing as he notices the woman in the window. She is sitting at her usual table: one leg crossed over the other, chin cupped in her palm, her big green eyes flickering back the red and white lights of the six o'clock traffic. She shows no sign of feeling watched.

When I go up to the Professor's table, he drags his eyes from her face to mine, and jiggles his eyebrows sug-gestively.

I try not to cringe, and ask him for his order.

'Time,' he says, nodding at the woman. 'Time for two please.'

'Sorry Prof, we're all out of Time here!'

'Ha!' he laughs—sudden and too loud. The woman at the window still shows no reaction. Red-faced but beaming, he asks for his usual and I leave him to stare.

'It's disgusting,' Mark says in the kitchen when I pass on the order. He is looking over my shoulder and out through the door's porthole. 'She knows she's being watched. She *comes here* to be watched.' He takes the docket off me, shaking his head. I don't say a word.

Back in the café, I get the Professor his glass of wine, set up his table and ask him what he's been teaching the kids. 'Earthquakes,' he says, tapping the table and pointing to the faint ripples on the surface of his wine. 'These men,' he says, 'can measure the tiniest vibrations.' He keeps tapping the table. 'The seismic waves of earth tremors—they're minute!' He looks up, smiling as he always does when he re-realises the phenomenal capabilities of his science. 'These men can measure *nothing.*'

'There's no such thing as nothing then, is there?' I say, flicking the side of his glass, making the wine ripple again.

'That's right!' He thumps the table. The glass jumps. 'There's no such thing as nothing!'

The bell rings from the kitchen. I turn to go. Stop. The woman in the window is looking straight at us, smiling.

Days like these are the days that matter. Mark still doesn't get it. He still shuns the gifts these people give us: there is no such thing as nothing; there is her smile of thanks.

Ø

I wanted a café, but it was Mark who wanted to live out here. He thought polluted worlds were killing him. He complained about industry. About graffiti on walls. Noise in the air. Chemicals in his lungs and cancer cells chain-reacting through his blood. He used Ash's death as evidence. I must have nodded in agreement. Maybe I was in shock. Somehow I forgot to tell him that polluted worlds were my home.

At night, Ash and I would climb a ladder and sit on the edge of our veranda's flat roof. Over our back fence lay a stretch of empty land full of weeds, burnt-out cars, dumped rubbish and upturned trolleys. This wasteland formed the buffer between our suburb and the frontier of the refineries. That place lit up at night: kilometres of white lights ordered into floating geometric patterns, their metal scaffolds invisible in the dark and the distance. 'Desolate' was the word. Huge and desolate. It seemed impossible that people made and ran that place. Impossible that the low hum throbbing from it was anything other than its own autonomous heartbeat. Ash and I felt privileged up there on the roof, like we were the only ones to have noticed—to dare admit—the profound beauty of this ecological destroyer.

I suppose to most people the refinery was an ugly thing. My cousins from the country would visit at Christmas and tease us about it. They said the chemicals in the air and the soil would give us three-eyed, two-headed babies. But I liked the smell of sulphur and oil. I liked the fingers of smoke and the sky-shimmer of steam and gas. 'The sun couldn't set like this,' Ash would say, 'without those chimneys.'

Later on, I'd find him sitting up on the veranda roof alone, his legs hanging over the edge, staring for hours at the night-matrix of lights. He would peer down at me, then invite me to join him—but by then I couldn't smile as usual, and climb the ladder as usual, to join him as usual. He understood. Some nights he'd get stuck up there, newly afraid of slipping. He'd call out for me. Then slowly, clumsily, I'd help him down the ladder, enclosing him between the rungs and my body, lifting and steadying his legs for him and moving his hands to the right places on the ladder's sides. I wanted to lift him. I felt like I could. In the cold white light of the refinery, the substance of his body really did seem to have liquefied and bled away. When we made it to the ground he'd always say, 'Sorry about that.' I hated how he apologised, as if things happened for reasons; as if what was happening to him was his fault.

When we first moved out here, Mark would go on and on about the beauty of this cliff side. Untouched beaches. Infinite horizons. Calm blue waters. Stormy grey seas. He kept trying to claim the landscape by describing it, as if desperate to deny what was obvious: words aren't made for places like this; places like this will always speak for themselves. One day, when he pronounced on the scenery again, I snapped at him: 'Beauty is boring.' He had no reply to that.

I don't find this landscape beautiful. Like the

Professor, I'm impressed by technology and industry, by the savage genius of our ability to humanise and dehumanise space. Factories, wharves, suburbs, highways, cities, tips, quarries, mines. These are the things I love, these monuments to our capacity to destroy and create with the very same gesture.

Sometimes at night, whilst listening to the too-regular breaths of Mark's fake-sleeping, a vision of the refinery evolves on our bedroom wall. It tears at my gut. Not because Ash is suddenly there, looking on alongside me. But because I miss that proof of life.

Here, away from the city lights, the night falls and everything disappears. It gets so dark, sometimes, that I cannot see my hand in front of my face. On nights like this I feel the blackness filling my eyes and ears and nose and mouth and lungs like syrup. I'll flick on the light before panic swamps me. Sooner or later Mark will flick it back off again. He says he likes how the dark erases his edges. He says that's what he came here for.

Ø

'They're leeches,' Mark says for the hundredth time. '*Leeches.*' He spits the word at me, as if I'm one too. He has just been cornered by Harry, one of the regulars who wants to—needs to—talk to us. Harry has dirty grey hair tied in a knot at his neck. He wears clothes that would be retro-cool if they weren't filthy and falling apart. He can't bear how the world has changed away from him, and we often get stuck at his table, audience to a perpetual monologue about his idealised youth. But he's not all clichés and self-absorption. I've watched him tap his fingers along to whatever music we have playing. I've seen him freeze like a meerkat. I've replayed endless tracks for him, at his request. And then I've watched as, just like the Professor, he fills napkin after napkin with scrawled messages to himself.

Once, when I cleared Harry's table, I picked one of these napkins up, hoping to souvenir it. He snatched it back, assuming I was going to throw it in the bin. 'Sorry,' he said, smoothing the creases out on the table. The napkin was covered in musical notation: the neat, perfectly spaced lines of staves, dotted with a chaos of notes. I smiled at it. He looked uncertain, as if unsure whether I was laughing at him or not. 'It's the chords,' he said, then hummed a tune under his breath, emphasising some sounds and speeding over the others. 'In some of these chords,' he pointed to a shape floating on the tissue, 'you can hear God.' Just as I do with the Professor and Mark, I nodded, pretending I understood. As I left his table, I recited his words in my head till they stuck.

Later, in the kitchen, I told Mark what Harry had said. Mark didn't look up. He just kept on working—as if I wasn't even in the room.

This afternoon the café is quiet, so I go and sit in the seat that Mark has just fled. Harry beams at me. Resumes his monologue. There is sugar spilled across his table: like the Professor, he always makes a mess. I listen whilst drawing patterns in the grains with the tip of my finger.

Silence. I look up. Harry is frowning at me. Then he dashes my patterns across the table with his hand, making me jump. Our eyes lock. He looks so very serious and so very, very kind. He says, 'You can *never* change the past. But you can *always* change how you feel about it.'

That body-jolt of recognition.

I nod. Then I apologise, stand, and get away as quickly as I can. I walk across the café to the kitchen, using those seconds to freeze my surging tears.

I pause at the door, composing myself. I see Mark through the glass porthole. He is resting against the sink. His arms are crossed. He stares at the floor.

My automatic impulse is to share Harry's gift of insight. I want to show Mark how we need these people as much as they need us. But I don't move. I know that he will just turn on me in anger. He'll sneer, 'Leech, loser, lost'. That's what he'll say. Then I will stare at him until my silence amplifies the fact that it is he—and he alone—who flinches at such words.

Mark looks up, sensing my gaze. Can he see what Harry has just seen? My history—our history—orbiting around me like Saturn's icy rings?

Mark suddenly grabs at the knots of his apron. Fumbles with the ribbons. Hauls the apron off. Dumps it on the steel counter and slams out the back door.

Ø

The next morning, as I twist the market umbrellas into their heavy bases, I see Mark wandering up the warped wooden stairs from the beach. His clothes are crumpled. His bare arms are crossed tightly over his chest, as if trying to squeeze out this ocean air that keeps expanding him with anticipation as he waits and waits and waits for his life to begin.

He will wander across the road. He will not look at me. He will take the umbrella from my hands and secure it to the table. He will finish putting up the other umbrellas, while I put out the salt and pepper and sugar. Together, we will bring out the heavy benches, and then we will go inside and sit in the window. We will read, silently. Our customers will turn up, as they always do, and the day will unfold, as it always does.

'You have to go,' my brother said, 'or you'll end up with nothing.'

Different kinds of repetition. Different kinds of nothing.

What there is. And what there isn't. Which, after all, is everything.

QUARRY

LUKE CROSSES HIS arms against the bluster and stares out across the grey. Even on the hottest days in summer, when dozens of people come here to walk their dogs or jog or fish or set up barbecues with their damn kids screaming everywhere, this bench just stands here empty. It seems to wait for him, as if his own name is gouged across its grain rather than Beck's and Ahmed's and Pete's and Shanae's. Luke hugs himself and squints through the gritty spray. A rock wall ties one side of the lake to the other, dividing the water in two. A man sits in the middle of the wall, in the middle of the lake, fishing. Luke watches him, then looks over him to the twisted white gums drowned along the far bank. He studies the gums, studies them hard.

He doesn't want to look at the idiot girl struggling

with a board and huge red kite on his side of the wall. Can't bear to watch her because, when he does, he sees her yanked under the chopped water. Sees her thrashing and sinking. Sees her wetsuit become heavier, slicker, blacker, bloated as she fights for the surface. Sees her stop. Stillness, silence. Feels the lake in her lungs. Watches her rise up again. Watches her tug to a halt, the ropes and pulleys of her harness tangled in the trash below. She's a human balloon, floating forever in the toxic grey silence.

Luke's gaze flickers between the fisherman and the gums and the cormorants striking ridiculous poses on the ashen branches. He thanks Christ that summer, with its swarms of people and its glare and its endless daylight hours, has finally come to an end.

A red flash. The kite is up, hovering. The girl thrusts herself backwards. With powerful jerks of her long thin arms she wrenches the parachute left and right till it cups the full force of the wind. She races across the raging water. Faster. Faster. White foam fans up as she grinds her weight down into the board, turning and speeding away from him. Now she's aiming straight at the rock wall. Faster. Closer. Too fast, too close. Only once she's cleared the wall—for somehow, with the smallest spring of her knees, she rises up, up into the air and flies right over it—does Luke realise he's holding his breath. He's furious with himself. He's furious with her, but cannot look away as she flashes across the far side of the lake. Back and forth she goes, gathering speed till—again and again—she launches herself into the sky where she turns in strangely slow, wind-borne pirouettes. When he leaves his bench to walk his afternoon loops, the wind still carries her. It carries her to him in the ebb and flow of her whoops and yells.

Later, as he trudges up the overgrown gravel path, he sees her. She walks further up the incline, dragging her gear in a big canvas bag. Despite the autumn chill, she's wearing denim shorts. Even in the low light, he can see her muscles shift under the smooth, tanned lengths of her legs. Through her yellow shirt, see-through from her dripping hair, he counts the knobbles of her spine. One, two, three. He coughs so she can hear his approach. Four, five, six. She stops and turns. Suddenly he's staring at her nipples jagging through the thin fabric. Tiny flat breasts, a boy's chest except for those nipples and the dark shadows showing faintly around them. He looks down. Sees the taut tendons of her bony ankles. Sees stars, scores of black stars tattooed across the tops of her feet. Looks up. Aqua eyes. Blonde lashed. Cool eyes in a face flushed from surfing, or from the icy wind, or from him—from being near him. She bites her lip. Gives him that rapid female assessment he's just so damned sick of. He stares at the gravel. She stands to one side, yanks her gear out of his way. Gives him a curt, 'Hi.' He nods, moves a few paces, stops near her, just below her. He feels his silence unloop within him, feels it stretch out to her, surrounding her like an arm, tugging her towards him. She looks away. Squints up ahead as if it's still sunny. As if she's calculating how long it will take to run up to the car park.

His voice lumps in his throat. 'It's not safe,' he says. He coughs. He points back to the scrub-hid lake. Steadily, she looks away. He steps forwards. Stops right next to her. 'It's not safe.' Still, she will not face him. Instead, she leans back slightly, so that a branch catches the hem of her sleeve, twisting the yellow fabric up into a tiny tepee. Suddenly, he sees them as if from above: a huge scarred man standing over a pretty blonde girl. A horror-movie man standing over a kid on a track in the middle of nowhere. If she screamed, he wonders, would they hear her up there, up there in the houses? If she ran, he wonders, could I catch her? And if I caught her, could I …? He coughs again, furious. Would I?

Whose thoughts are these! (Torture, to sense it, the fear pulsing from her.) Whose thoughts are these! (Agony, to see it, the fear bitten down in those thin, pale lips.) Whose thoughts are these! (Horror, to feel it, something stirring, stirring deep within him.) He storms up the gravel away from her. He slams out the gate into the dusky roads that enclose the old quarry and its flooded gut. Christ. *Christ*. I only wanted to warn her, didn't I? I only wanted to ask her—did I? didn't I?—what it's like to fly.

Ø

Cane strides straight into the kitchen. Luke feels the shorter man's eyes fix on the ruined side of his face. It's your turn today, big shot. That's what Cane's saying without saying a word. Everyone understands. Luke senses Charlie and Dave stumble in their prepping on either side of him: their pity and relief that, today, it's him and not them. Feels the shift in Quang's back-turned muteness at the sink—a vibration, changing in the air. Luke keeps his eyes on his hands—huge, one scar-wrapped from nail to wrist—which continue their work without flinch or pause. For the thousandth time he wonders at the disconnect that must lie within him, allowing him to keep working no matter how his mind rebels. Though he's endured a hundred humiliations in a dozen bastards' kitchens, though he knows the banal predictability of these rituals, and though he finally understands that these rituals say nothing about him—and everything about them—Luke still rages. He holds steady on the outside, but fumes on the inside, knowing he'll waste hours tonight replaying what is about to happen, rehearsing it for how it could and should have been instead.

And here it goes. There's Cane lifting one of Luke's perfect breakfasts, asking, 'What the *fuck* is this?' There's Cane's stubby finger jabbing at the silky white skin of a poached egg. There's the yolk spurting across the gleaming ceramic. There's Sarah appearing over Cane's shoulder. Her immediate recognition of the scene. Her immediate, empty-handed, return to the café. There's the scuff of Miriam's footsteps stopping near the doorway. The pause of her listening. The brisk *tap tap tap* of her retreat. There's the chatter of the café lulling as Cane's rant escalates: 'Fuck this. Fuck that. Fuck fuck *fuck*.' There's Luke hearing Charlie—tiny Charlie, their head bloody chef—choking on her breath like a child. There's Dave trying to curl all six feet of his gawky eighteen-year-old body into his concave chest. And worst of all, there's Luke, just standing there and taking it. Taking it as he knows he must. Taking it while Cane's face twists in on itself like an arsehole gotten stuck on something. There's Luke, trying not to laugh, thinking: An arsehole with the face of an arsehole. There's the urge to laugh dissolving as he wonders why he must take it, why all of them must take it, always, always.

Suddenly, he's acutely aware of the sheer volume of his own blood pumping through the powerful machinery of his flesh as Cane—a man Luke could crush with one fist—grabs his two beautifully finished meals. A curiously intimate squish as Cane stacks the plates, one on top of the other. The clatter as he throws the meals into the bin, plates and all. Now Cane's at Luke's shoulder. 'Make them again, *hot shot*.' Immediately, Luke obeys. As steady as ever, his hands remake the meals while his brain reminds his raging core that no-one will ever take this from him. No-one will ever take away his satisfaction at making something from nothing. At making wholeness from scattered parts. At knowing his creation is desired by someone. That his fingerprints—even the muted blanks of his bad hand—will travel over their lips and into their bodies. There's Cane shaking his head at

Luke's remade meals. Cane playing the lead in his theatre of disgust. Cane thumping the bell, clicking his fingers at Sarah and Miriam as they hurry down the hall from the café. Cane passing Charlie's nerve-wrecked Benedict to Miriam, his cool voice saying, 'Here, sis.' There's Miriam, averting her face from her brother's, her eyes already puffing up as she hurries the meals back into the café. There's Cane passing Luke's meals to Sarah, 'Here, sweetie.' And then there's Sarah's gold-speckled eyes. Sarah, staring her anger and sympathy and understanding straight into Luke so that he curses his body—for, though he knows what he is (a big man, boiling, boiling, boiling), he knows how he looks (a big man blushing, blushing like a fucking girl).

Cane follows Sarah into the café. Everyone listens, tracking his movements. No, he doesn't leave. He's not done yet. He's coming back. He storms by the servery window to the tiny office at the back of the building. Miriam soon follows, hurrying past, head down.

Slowly, the kitchen returns to its usual rhythm. No-one says a word—and what is there to say, anyway? They work through the orders that have piled up since Cane appeared. As Luke prepares each meal, he damns the lot of them. He damns Cane, that animal who keeps them all in work. He damns poor, stupid Miriam, Cane's sister, who fears him and depends on him more than anybody else. He damns the loaded, watching silence of Quang. He damns Charlie and her manic moods—one day you're her babe, the next day you're a cunt—and he damns the world for the bruises all over her. ('From kickboxing,' she says. 'From kicking some sweet bitch *ass*,' she says each time, laughing, as if everyone can't see what's happening to her.) He even damns shy and gentle Dave, the most useless apprentice Luke's ever had to train. And of course Luke damns Sarah. He damns her to hell for the way she doesn't flinch at the mess of his scars. For the way her strange eyes seek his. For how she always tries to talk to him. Most of all he damns her for the low, husky songs she sings each night as she cleans up the café out front. He's never heard a voice like hers. He can't decide if he likes it or loathes it, sure only of its power to lodge in his head so that her eyes and face and body—and her sweaty cinnamony smell—follow him home each evening.

Luke keeps working, dreading what awaits him. For he knows that, alone in his bed tonight, he'll be killing Cane and fucking Sarah. That's what he'll be doing. And he damns himself for this, for his pathetic fantasies, for his sordid, fucked-up dreams that feed his nights and paralyse his days.

Ø

Luke sits on his bench, chips spread out on butcher's paper across his knees keeping him warm. He breathes in the eye-watering steam of vinegar, sucking it up with the sweet background rot of the leaf litter and the lake's silty shallows. He's been cheffing for decades but, still, nothing beats this: greasy hot chips, eaten outside.

He's watching the night roll in on the back of another storm, hoping those mad black clouds will blot out this morning's humiliation. There's no-one around. No kitesurfer, though it's windy as hell. No joggers. Not even the usual dog walkers. He'd normally be home by now too, but he just can't muster himself tonight. He's sick of his flat, of floating between the TV and the kitchen and all that filthy shit online that he just can't look away from. Sick of white noise. Of watching his life shoot backwards in time, streaking away from him, leaving nothing behind. Is that why he started these walks? Did he really think the grip of his shoes on the ground would help him get a grip on the newly gaping hours of his nights and bloody endless Sundays? Idiot. Stupid, to have quit the restaurant after so many years. Stupid, to think working café-shaped days instead of restaurant-filled nights—working 'normal hours'— would make *him* normal too.

Luke discovered the lake by accident. A few months ago, at the beginning of summer, he'd stepped out of his unit for his usual late-afternoon wander and found himself halted at the sidewalk. His body was protesting. It refused to trace another lap of the gridlocked houses and shops near his home. Instead, it pointed him towards the industrial planes on the other side of the freeway. He'd never paid much attention to this area. It was unpopulated, polluted and ugly, but as he walked he felt his mind begin to unwind into the stark streets. Strange, how that concrete landscape welcomed him in a way that the domestic monotony of his suburb never had. And so he kept wandering until a fence dead-ended his path. He stood there, in long yellow grass. Saw how the fence's barbed-wire curl glittered for kilometres towards and away from him, marking a divide between the backs of the industrial estates on one side, and an endless stretch of scrub on the other. He pointed himself towards the distant refinery, kept walking. His curiosity dwindled when the estates ended and the freeway's twenty-foot-high, corrugated soundproofing rose up in their place. It was hot. He knew he could walk for hours and get nowhere. It was only luck that saw him come across the gate before deciding to turn back home. He shouldered it open and found himself on an overgrown dirt path. As he walked, a wall of earth slowly rose to his left, its surface scarred with worn, down-thrust gouges. On his right, a few feet from his shoes, the ground dropped to another path below which, he soon realised, was his own path circling back on itself. He was descending the rough-hewn shelves of an old open-earth cutting. Down he went, picking his way over dusty weeds and tree roots until the path suddenly flattened out. And there it was. The lake. His lake. A vast stretch of water cut in two by a wall of black rocks.

It unnerved him. All that water in the drought. All those birds and trees and reeds—all that life—claiming a hole cut into a wasteland. All of this just kilometres from his home, but completely unknown to him.

Since that night, Luke has returned to the lake most

evenings. He often drives here straight from the café, parking by the fence at the top. It's been raining for a month, and the water has finally turned from algal pink to milky grey. Though the days are getting shorter, Luke still traces a distorted figure eight around the lake's two halves most nights. If no-one's around, he stands in the middle of the rock wall and closes his eyes. Sometimes he loses balance and stumbles, sure that the rocks are about to crack open and suck him down into watery depths. Other times he stands steady, his momentary blindness magnifying the sounds around him. The drip and slap of water. The moronic muttering of the birds. The endless drone of the freeway. The crisp rustle of the gums. On these days he shuts his eyes and lets the sounds press in on him, a thousand tiny hands holding him up like a column of stone.

It's getting late. His leftover chips have gone cold and starchy. Luke doesn't want to go home to his unit. There's nothing for him there. But he also doesn't want to be around when the kids arrive. He's seen them a dozen times now. Most Friday and Saturday nights they race through the dusk in their utes, swerving down the single steep road that ties the lake to the edge of the suburbs. Their cars are nothing like his dad's old ute, that rusted monster that ploughed them through the bush around the farm all those years ago. These kids have the same spotlights and roll bars, but their cars are built for speed, painted for show: flashy V8s sprayed in metallic greens and reds and golds. Luke's not really sure what their cars are designed for, and he can't place the kids either. The older guys are in their twenties. They're clean-cut, but covered in tatts and all bulked up, like they've stepped out of a gym. They remind him of Cane: smooth and cashed up and hard. There's something primitive about them; something corporate too. The younger ones are just kids, awkward in hoodies and caps and jeans. They remind him of Dave, and of Miriam's son, Jamie. There's something soft about them; something pathetic. Luke realises these kids probably look just like he and his mates did, twenty years ago, when they drove out to the dam to drink and turn tricks in the dust till the air smoked. Whoever they are, Luke avoids them. He's not scared of them. He just assumes that they, like he, want to be left alone.

Luke sits up and shifts the cold, greasy papers from his lap onto the bench. He makes to stand. Stops. A sound. Something snaps in the shrubbery. He stares into the dark bushes. No sound. No movement. Slowly, he sits back. He reaches for the chips and begins to scrunch them into their papers. Keeps watching the shadows. Another sound: something pressing softly into the leaf litter. He can barely hear it. Something dark, upsetting the darkness. He can barely see it. He freezes. Feels the shadow size him up. A shimmer. A momentary flash of white. Teeth. A black dog slinks into the clearing. It pads towards him, its head and body lowered, its huge ears cupping and turning like radars. It stops a few metres from him. Raises its pointed muzzle. Sniffs him out.

Luke knows better than to return a dog's stare. He looks over it, around it. He slowly places the paper-wrapped chips on his lap. Tries to stay calm though his blood thickens and thuds in his ears. He hates dogs. He saw too many of them go feral on the farm. He loved hunting them down. Loved that clean, quick rip as he tore their scalps from their skulls for the rangers. What was it back then? Ten bucks for a fox's and fifty for a dog's because the dogs were different. They didn't kill for food. They killed for fun. At first Luke had enjoyed the chase, and he'd hang their bodies from the gums as a fly-struck warning to the others. He was proud of his work. But his pride stuttered within him as the landscape began to fill with dog trees. Then dog fences. The more dogs they killed, the more seemed to appear. He'll never forget that night on the back tracks. He'd pulled over to let a trapper pass in his ute. Unforgettable, the stench. Tragic, that man's face, its stoic lines carved deep with orange dust, exaggerated and distorted by Luke's bright head-lights. The man nodded as he passed, dozens of dead dogs strapped to his tray. That was when Luke realised they weren't playing a game. They were fighting a war.

Luke monitors the black dog sidelong as these old images reel through him. He tries to read the animal's intent from its body. He can't. All he can do is notice its huge ears. Its small face. Its broad ribs rippling up to a tiny waist. Long skinny legs. Huge paws. Puppy paws, perhaps, but a neck and chest as broad and muscled as any fighting dog's. A true mongrel. The dog takes a tentative step closer. Noses the air. Raises one of its front legs in the pointer's archetypal pose. A hunter? Fighter? Racer? A working dog?

Again, it inches forwards. Luke raises his hands. The animal freezes. Its hackles flare. A low grumble sounds from deep within its chest. It plants its feet firmly in the dirt: braced. Luke doesn't move. Seconds pass like minutes. The dog begins to relax. It noses towards Luke again, its long thin tail curled over its spine like a question mark. Luke looks at the dog's jut of ribs. Remembers the discarded chips. Carefully picks the papers up. Again, the hackles flare. Another low growl meets Luke's movement and the papers' crunch. Luke realises his hands—his ever-steady hands—are shaking, and suddenly it's all too much. He stands. The chips drop onto the dirt. The dog bolts back into the bushes. Luke waits, breath held. But there is no sound. No movement. The animal is gone.

Eventually, Luke kicks the rubbery chips across the ground. He retrieves the papers and wanders back up the circling path. By the time he reaches the gate he is calm enough to be slapped again by the memory of Sarah witnessing his pathetic role in Cane's pantomime. Forget it, he tells himself. Just forget it, forget it, forget it. Only when he reaches his car does he hear the faint rev of utes across the lake. The squeal of their tyres pierces the darkness, mapping the kids' suicidal swerve down, down, down into the quarry's flooded gut.

Ø

Luke and Quang are cleaning up the kitchen. They don't talk. Sarah's low singing drifts in from the café where she sweeps and wipes and wraps up food. Accompanying her, the muffled coin-clatter and odd self-chatter of Miriam counting out the till in the office. At this time of day, Cane is never around and Charlie and Dave are usually both long gone. At this time of day, even the most lingering customers have disappeared and so the four of them can relax, each working efficiently and quietly, getting everything done without anyone telling anyone what to do.

Screaming.

The quiet steels to silence.

Silence and screaming.

Silence and screaming.

Luke's scars ripple with recognition. He's heard these screams before. They thrust him back two decades, back to his first job in his first kitchen when his own arm and face sizzled in oil because some crazy cunt thought he'd show him who's boss. For two decades he's tried to forget it and for two decades his skin's phantom mind has clung to what happened: screams of agony and terror; the blinding horror of seeing skin melt off skin.

Look up. Look up.

Luke sees Quang dancing in the middle of the kitchen. Tiny Quang—red-faced and screaming—is dancing. He's hopping up and down. His long black ponytail swings from left to right like something from a bad slapstick comedy. Why is he dancing? Just like

221

a movie, Luke feels everything slow down. Vaguely, he registers the same stupid torpidity in Miriam and Sarah's silence.

Luke sees that the mop bucket is overturned by Quang's feet. Sees the floor gone strange. Flooded and shining. Gleaming and steaming. Sees hot water lapping at the edges of his own rubber clogs. Looks from his clogs to Quang's runners. Sees how they don't steam from their soles, as his own do. Sees them steam from their tops, from their laces. Says to himself: Quang's feet are boiling. Quang's feet are trapped. Luke knows he must act. Instead, he stares and wonders, Why is Quang in lace-ups? I *told* Miriam to get him clogs, didn't I?

Then, everything happens at once.

He is slip-running across the wet floor. He's grabbing Quang by the arm. He's dragging him down the hall and out the back. He's throwing him onto the concrete. He hears himself yelling, 'Hose, hose, hose!' Sees his hands struggle with hot laces. The strangeness of that image: his gentleness; his brutal scars. Notes pain in his fingertips. Ignores it. Eases Quang's runners and socks off. Quang screams with every movement. Magically, a hose appears by Luke's shoulder. He grabs it. Runs the freezing stream over each of Quang's feet. One then the other. One then the other.

It takes an age for Quang to stop crying. To stop reciting those same three Vietnamese words. (What do they mean? Who are they for?) Finally, Quang is silent. He lies on the flooded concrete, propped up on his elbows. Stunned and sodden, he stares down at the newborn weals that have pinked his feet.

Luke glances over his shoulder to see who gave him the hose. Miriam stands with one hand covering her mouth. Her other hand clenches a fistful of T-shirt at her waist. She looks like she is about to be sick. Sarah stands next to her, arms loose by her sides, expressionless. The low winter sun has transformed them. The gold flecks in Sarah's irises glow, as if she is lit from within. Even her hair shines warmly, though it's as black as ever. And Miriam seems different too. Her frizzy red hair flames around her soft, round face—a cartoonist's halo. He senses their reality as never before. Their living, tangible, utterly female bodies. These two women of warmth, of flesh, of blood, of mind—of life, of life, of life—making his own body roar, making him feel the reality of *his* warm flesh, *his* maleness, *his* livingness.

What the hell is wrong with me? he thinks, pushing down the waves of desire that are pulsing through him. Somehow, he turns back to Quang's raw feet. Calls, 'Ambulance. Ambulance.' When no-one moves, he turns around again.

The sun has dipped below the buildings on the other side of the lane. Miriam and Sarah look normal. Miriam stares down at him, her face blotching with red. 'No,' she says, her voice as monotone as the dwindling light. She shakes her head. '*No.*' Her voice quivers, almost inaudible. As her refusal drifts into the dusk, she turns away. Gazes at the garbage bins shoved along the back fence. 'Cane,' she mutters. She shrugs, as if that's expla-nation enough. Finally she turns back to Luke. A terrible face. All that sadness. All that fear. All her strength and weakness.

Sarah disappears into the café.

Luke turns back to Quang, restraining himself. He will hit Miriam. He will belt her until she says, 'Yes, of course we'll get help, *of course* we will.' He tries to concentrate on Quang, who is silent, staring at his feet through the strands of long black hair that are stuck to his face with snot and tears and sweat.

Soon, Sarah reappears with towels and a hotchpotch of clothes. She helps Quang hobble to the bathroom. She closes the door behind him, turns, crosses her arms and leans back against it. She's a sentinel, a guardian. Luke only glances at her for a moment, but long enough to see that he has misread her. She isn't expressionless. Her face mirrors his. Disbelief. Anger. A knot of self-control.

Only when Luke stands does he realise how stiff and wet and cold he is. He struggles to straighten himself. Everything hurts. His head hammers. He walks past Miriam and Sarah without looking at them. He returns to the kitchen and mops up the congealing grey slick on the floor. He potters around until he hears Sarah leave. Realises Quang is leaving with her. Jealousy drenches him, unexpected and total. He wanders into the café, finishes Sarah's work. By the time he goes to the office for his jacket, it's getting dark. He's suddenly desperate to get to the quarry and walk away the day—walk away from Quang's screams, from Sarah's care—but as he nears the closed door he slows. Stops in the hallway. It isn't the first time he's heard Miriam cry in there. She's always crying in there. Stupid Miriam, he thinks. Stupid Miriam with your fucked-up life and your fucked-up family—you fucking coward. Again he wants to hit her, as if weakness can be beaten out of a person.

Luke steps quietly back from the door. Silence. He turns, then, and hurries through the shop. Ignores the sound of the door flying open behind him. Ignores Miriam's high voice calling out to him, 'Luke? Luke!' He stumbles into the cold, bright street and slams into his car and drives straight to the quarry—his lake—her raw voice pursuing him. 'I'm sorry. I'm sorry, Luke! Don't tell Cane. *Luke?*'

Ø

Though he's not built for running, Luke jogs by the water. He pounds his feet into the dirt, pushing himself as hard as he can. And it works. The pain—Quang's screams from hours ago, his own screams from decades ago—shifts from his head to his shins. He pushes and pushes until he has to stop. Only then, bent with his hands on his knees and gasping, does he see the black dog across the water. It stands in the middle of the rock wall. Its tail and nose are lifted. It's a picture-perfect cut-out against the lake's low gleam. A living silhouette.

After that first night with the chips, nearly a month ago, Luke became sensitised to the dog's presence. He somehow knew when it was following him. Somehow knew that it had followed him all along. When he'd sense the dog near him, he would stare straight ahead and try to beat up a tattoo of distraction with his feet, just as he is tonight. But the rhythm only gave momentum to the words circling inside him. It's stalking me, I'm being stalked. It's stalking me, I'm being stalked. He'd speed up and stare forward, straining all of his senses to track the animal's proximity and to work out when—just as randomly—it had disappeared back into the shadows.

The animal's presence was bad enough, but worse were the half-buried memories it awakened. One memory in particular: the huge brindle-coated dog from his final weeks on the farm. That monster he shot at, lost sight of, but then found later by the dam, its muzzle bubbling blood. Always, the look in its glassy eyes as he placed his foot firmly on its skull. What was it? Terror? Defiance? Rage? Those eyes shone keenly. They looked and Luke looked back. He saw that the dog saw him. He saw the dog thinking something—*something*—as it stared up at him till the very second he jammed his great weight downwards and shut its gurgled whining up forever.

Worse than these images, though, is the surge of feelings that come with them. Feelings he thought he'd left on the farm. Feelings he thought two decades in a dozen kitchens had quelled. Those sickening, electrifying feelings that flooded him with all the revenge and mercy that made up the everyday of his father's work. Luke had hated it—and he had loved it—how they were gods out there. Perhaps that's why he left. Once the dogs took possession of the landscape—so that even his dad got nervous in the back paddocks, sure that the dogs or their ghosts were hunting *him*—Luke realised they would never be gods again.

The black dog stalked Luke for nearly a week before it re-emerged from the shrubs. At first Luke tried to face it off. He yelled, kicked stones, lunged as if to strike. At first the dog braced and bristled. Flared its hackles. Growled and snarled and snapped at the air before disappearing back into the bushes. But they soon sensed each other's bluff. Curiosity surpassed fear. The dog increasingly replied to Luke's charades with little more than a cartoonish tilt of its big-eared head and a slow, low swipe of its tail. That swipe became a wag and that wag has become a whole body wiggle that launches the dog at Luke's face, no matter how often he tries to knee it away. After the dog greets Luke like this, it trots calmly by his side, occasionally nose-butting his leg or nipping at his fingertips and always, always looking up at him with its clear amber eyes.

Once they began walking together, Luke found himself distracted at the café: every time he threw out food he saw the dog's laddered ribs. Though he knew it was his chips—the dog's hunger—that had lured it from the darkness on that first night, he didn't want to feed it. Didn't want to make a pet of it. And so he didn't understand why, one afternoon, he began wrapping up scraps of meat at the end of his shift. He took that greasy package straight to the lake, butterflies turning in him as he drove. The dog appeared within minutes. For once it forgot its jolly jumped greeting. Instead, it walked straight up to him, head-on. Luke tried to keep walking, but the dog wouldn't let him pass. It stood right in front of him, wide-eyed and agitated. It stared intensely at his face. It rose up onto its hind legs and sniffed the air. 'Okay,' Luke muttered. 'Okay!' But he didn't feel okay as he reached for his jacket pocket. Didn't feel okay as he noticed, again, the genetic triumph of muscle that knotted through the dog's neck and shoulders despite the skin and sinew and bone of its ribs and legs. As he unwrapped the meat, the dog began to pace. Its eyes flickered between Luke's hands and face. 'Here,' Luke said. He flicked a strip of fat at the dog's feet. The dog leapt. Grabbed it. Scuttled back. Dropped it. Sniffed it. Scoffed it, staring at Luke the entire time. 'Here,' Luke said, throwing another strip. Repeatedly, the dog grabbed, retreated, dropped, sniffed, scoffed, stared. One scrap left. Luke placed the meat on his palm. He squatted down. Held out his hand. He had no idea what he was doing. Or why.

The animal stared long and hard at that final scrap of food. Only once did its eyes flick up at Luke's face before returning again to the meat. In those stretched seconds, Luke felt the dog's body as if it was his own. He recognised the depth of its yearning. The pain of its longing.

A white flash of canines in a black velvet face.

The blur of large clawed paws.

A violent knock backward.

A flurry of vision and sensation—strength and softness all at once—as the dog grabbed the meat and disappeared into the scrub.

Just a dog. Just a dog. Yet, driven by its desire—its need—as powerful as any man.

Finally, Luke picked himself up off the ground. He was furious at himself for his carelessness, and furious at the dog for leaving him sprawled in the dirt. But as he walked back to his car, his anger turned in on itself. For what, exactly, had he expected? The dog had only done what he'd provoked it to do. And it had done so without leaving a scratch or slobber upon him. If the dog was a starved ball of muscle, it was also a master of restraint.

Tonight is the first time Luke has seen the dog before it has seen him. He gazes across the lake at it poised on the rock wall. Watches it sniff the air. Watches it pivot and begin to run towards the far bank. He has never seen the dog from a distance like this. He has never seen it run. He cannot look away. He suddenly recognises the perfection of its mongrel body. Suddenly sees what it is made for. As the dog gathers speed its paws blur into a sprint. It's a bird, a black bird, a raven, a crow, a bat swooping long and low and smooth into the thick wooded shadows of the quarry's gut. Luke starts walking in the same direction. He begins to run, suddenly eager to find the animal before it finds him, but as he speeds up, pain darts through his shin. He tries to ignore it. It gets worse. He's torn something. Twisted something. Idiot, he thinks, wincing and stopping. Idiot, to have run so hard. Stupid, to think a body can outrun its brain, outpace its pain.

Luke wanders back to his bench. He stares up into the clear night. Picks out the few constellations that his dad taught him. Orion's Belt. The Cross, of course. He struggles to find any other. He misses country skies. Skies where there's as much light as dark. Skies that make you small, your problems smaller. Though the pain in his shin has dulled, Luke's whole body aches from kneeling with Quang. The prospect of walking up to his car only makes him slump. He tells himself to get a grip. Then he senses it. The dog. He listens. He tries to work out where it is. He can't. It's as if the animal's gaze surrounds him. As if the dog itself is the lake, the dirt, the scrub and the rough-cut cliffs of the quarry's encircling paths. He waits. Soon enough the dog slinks out from the bushes near the water's edge, just as it did on that first night. It wiggle-wags up to him, head lowered. It nose-butts his folded arms, nuzzles his pockets. Luke holds up his empty hands. The dog sniffs and licks his fingers. When it realises that there's no food, it doesn't wander away as it normally would. Instead, after a pause, it steps in closer to him. It sits on the dirt between his feet. It just sits there, staring up at him, its warm, muscular body gently leaning into his sore leg. Luke slowly raises one of his hands. Their eyes remain locked as Luke's fingers move up and over its bony brow and lower onto its soft, soft skull.

This is the first time that Luke has initiated contact with the dog. This is the first time he's wanted to touch the animal simply for the sake of touching it. And the dog lets him. It lets him scratch the base of its ears. Lets his hand move under its chest and knead the muscles of its broad shoulders and neck. Lets his hand rest on the jarring corrugations of its ribs. All the while it stares into Luke's eyes. He feels the dog lean heavier into his leg until it suddenly collapses onto the dirt, belly up. It holds its front paws close to its chest—keeping its balance—while its back legs spread out, loose and floppy. Luke suddenly realises that it is a she. How could he not have noticed? Not have cared?

She's not worried. It's not she who flinches as he leans down to pat her thin-haired belly. It's not she who's stupidly embarrassed by her blatant genital exposure. He pats her tummy and looks elsewhere. At her ridiculous thrown-back grin. At the huge white canines and massive neck that once made him so nervous. He strokes her like this until she flips herself upright and trots away into the quarry's dark. Off she goes, leaving him alone with the ache of his legs and the tickle of his scars and the too-familiar sound of Quang's screams.

Ø

Luke stops when he sees them. Quietly, he moves to one side of the path and stands behind a tree. It's late. It's dark. He's not sure if he should carry on past them or turn back.

He's spent hours, tonight, looping around the lake. Spent hours hoping the cold will soothe his burning scars because, since Quang's accident last week, they have prickled back to life. He's already tried to calm himself in his usual way. He stood on the rock wall at dusk. Shut his eyes. Begged the music of the water and the birds and gums to fill him, hold him up. But tonight the world just shrank away from him. Eyes screwed shut, he felt the sounds recede instead of come close. Felt the lake begin to circle him. Faster. Faster. Thousands of litres of black ice spinning around him. Transforming him. A blind dot in the heart of a whirlpool. Opened his eyes. Regained his balance. Continued walking his loops. He went around once. Then again. And now his third loop has been interrupted by three utes parked right where his path crosses the gravel road.

Their open trays point towards the sparkling water. Seven or eight guys lounge against the cars. Talking. Drinking. Even though it's cold enough for ribbons of steam to ghost up from the centre of the lake, most of the kids are wearing T-shirts and jeans. One of the guys wraps a massive arm around the only girl who's there. They've lit a bonfire, and the girl's blonde hair and shiny pink jacket glow in the flames' flicker. Blonder than blonde. Pinker than pink. Her bare feet swing back and forth over the edge of the ute's tray. Two boys, much younger than the rest, sit on the ground next to the fire.

Both hug their knees. One pokes a stick into the flames, prodding the wood until a sharp crack silences the group. They watch as a thousand sparks Catherine-wheel into the night, curling up with the smoke. They're just kids, Luke tells himself. Just kids.

Something silver suddenly arcs from one of the utes towards the fire. Luke freezes. The boy with the stick swears and falls to one side. Clumsily he sits himself up, rubbing his hooded head. He looks over at the others. 'Fuck *off*,' he says. He grabs the can and hurls it back, but misses the ute by metres. The men laugh. One of them rushes at the kid. The boy flinches, covering his head with his arms. The man grabs his elbows and jerks him backwards. The kid's legs kick forwards, into the fire, scuffing up more sparks and smoke. The man drags the boy away. Jumps on top of him. Rips off his own T-shirt. Beats his hard and hairless chest. Yodels. Lays into the kid's stomach.

Luke retreats further into the shadows. Stops when he notices the girl whisper something to her guy. Watches her take his hand and put it up her skirt. Watches her grab at his crotch with her free hand. Watches her yank roughly. Luke flinches. Flinches and goes hard. The man hits her arm away, laughing. Then he isn't laughing. He's pushing himself off the tray. He's turning to her, throwing her backwards; everyone freezes at the muted thud of her head. Silence. He climbs back onto the tray and pins the girl down. One of his hands presses her wrists to the metal floor above her head. He shoves his knee between her legs. The others move away. One of them wolf-whistles and gropes the man in front of him. Pretends to hump his arse. More laughter and swearing. They gather around the man and boy who have resumed wrestling by the fire. Someone grabs the other kid and drags him into the scrum. Everyone laughs and begins laying into each other, the fire flaring and dimming as they move back and forth.

Luke takes another step back. He watches the guy in the ute fumble with his jeans. Watches his big, golden-lit arse shove into the girl. Watches her ankles lock behind his waist so her legs rock back and forth in time with his shoving rhythm, her hips bare and braced and wrenched up to meet him.

It's only when Luke turns away that he notices the black dog. She stands on the other side of the path, her coat catching snatches of firelight. She glances at him for a moment, her long tail swinging its usual, casual, hello. Then she turns back to the kids and the fucking and the fire, nosing the cool air, her huge ears mapping the scene. That's the last thing he sees as he hurries away. The dog, perfectly outlined against the fire-lit glow of the cutting.

It's not until much later, in bed, that he makes the connection. It's not until then, when he's hot and sticky and feeling—as he always does afterwards—exposed and pathetic and so damn alone, that he realises who she is. The girl fucking—being fucked—in the ute (the same girl who's just grabbed his cock and pulled him

into her and wrapped her legs around him, around *him*)
is the girl with the kite. The girl who could fly. The girl
with the night sky tattooed across her feet.

Ø

As far as Luke knows, no-one has asked about Quang.
When Cane appeared earlier this week, he was in a rare
good mood, banging on about his imminent overseas
trip as he worked alongside Luke through lunch. He
didn't even notice the new dishwasher: a miserable git
that Miriam poached from the pub up the road. When
Charlie saw him she simply shook her head and muttered, 'Fucking dishies. Fucking *useless*.' The sour old
shit turned and stared at her, looking grey-faced and
bored as hell. Dave looked up, apparently just realising
that Quang was gone. All Luke knows is that Miriam
gave Sarah an envelope the day after the accident. Help
money. Or hush money. Probably both. Seeing that,
he'd felt another absurd joust of jealousy. Had to remind
himself, She's just a waitress, just a workmate. I'm
nothing to her. Nothing.

Miriam stops by the servery window. Sarah appears
next to her, proclaiming, 'Freedom!' Everyone laughs.
It's hard to ignore the relief—the lightness—that per-
meates the café now that Cane is finally off on his trip
to Europe. Charlie is singing under her breath, despite
seeming subdued and troubled all week. Dave is whistling as he sorts through the salad mix. He's trying to
ignore Sarah and Miriam who are teasing him about

his new girlfriend. Dave turns redder and redder. His whistling becomes breathy, stops. He disappears into the cool room, but there's only so long he can hide in there. When he reappears they immediately resume their attack. 'Okay!' he says, sounding mad but unable to keep the smile off his face as he takes out his phone to show everyone a photo.

When Luke sees it, Dave transforms into a stranger. He is no longer the quiet, incompetent kid he and Charlie have been struggling to train all year. The girl in the picture is young. Pretty in the way that all kids are pretty, though—from the way she is wrapped up in Dave—she is clearly extraordinary to him. And he to her. Dave holds the phone out for Luke, assuming correctly that he won't stop his work to study it closely like everyone else. Luke glimpses the photo. Feels the tightness of his own smile. Turns quickly away, overwhelmed by Dave's shy pride and his obvious desire for approval.

Luke knows Dave likes him. But that doesn't count for much. The young ones always do. After their initial shock at the sight of him, they learn to trust him. They see that he'll answer their questions without making them feel stupid. That he won't yell at them. That he doesn't push people around. That he'll take whatever bullets are flying around the kitchen because he and they both know that a man with scars like his can't get hurt the way they still can. Anyhow, it's easy to like someone who's not a threat, isn't it? For who feels threatened by someone they pity? 'Freak,' he heard one waitress say a long, long time ago. 'Poor freak,' she'd said. Then she'd giggled to her friend, 'When d'you reckon was the last time *he* got laid?' Luke had wanted to kill her. And himself. Back then, his wounds were still raw with healing, and the torment of never getting laid consumed him totally. But even though he wanted to hurt her, or flee, he recognised the odd mix of pity and affection in her voice. The same mix that was in Miriam's voice when he first started at the café, when he heard her whisper to Sarah, 'What's his story, poor guy?' They could have asked him. They didn't. They haven't. No-one ever does. Not that he blames them. And he sure can't blame Dave for showing off his new girl. And so, forced to face that photo, Luke does his best to nod and smile and ignore the growing silence. He says nothing. He just keeps working until their unasked question—You gotta girl, Luke?—merges into jokes about dick warts and HIV, G-spots and Brazilians, marriage and babies.

Soon, Miriam and Sarah disappear back into the café. Everyone in the kitchen gets busy with the first lunch orders. As Luke works, their unasked question pursues him. You gotta girl, Luke? You had a girl, Luke? What will he reply if anyone asks him? Must he point to his face, his arm, his size? To his fucked-up body? A body that even grown men flinch at the sight of? No-one in the world—except bloody Sarah—can hold his gaze. They either stare at his mauled eyelid as if, underneath, his eye's as blind as a marble, or they look quickly away and never look back. And even if someone did want him, the idea of a girl crooked in his shredded arm makes him sick. Imagine, a clear smooth cheek against his skin's knitted warps. Horrible. Imagine, soft plump lips—anyone's lips—pressed into his gnarled face. Disgusting.

But worse than these imaginings is knowing that no-one had ever wanted him anyway, not even before he got wrecked. He was always too big. Too awkward. Too quiet. A country kid. Always one of the boys. Never one with the girls. And the few times he'd had a chance, he fucked everything up. He didn't know what to do. The girls laughed at him. They fled from him. They froze him out. Somehow it was his fault when things went wrong, though all they ever did was lie there and do nothing—*nothing*—yet expected everything! He still has no idea what to do, and all the sordid shit he's filled his body's void with has just made it worse. Made it impossible. The fact is, he's almost grateful that cunt ruined him all those years ago. At least now he can blame his scars for why he hasn't, can't, won't. And it's too late now, he tells himself. It's too late. I've left everything for too damn long.

Wednesday is always busy, and by the end of the lunchtime rush Charlie is in a good mood. Perhaps it's the adrenaline of trying to keep up, or the relief of Cane's absence, or simply time's distance from whatever's been hanging over her this week. Whatever it is, Luke knows she's feeling better when she flicks on the radio and starts jiving her hard little body around the kitchen. Soon she's chatting about her boxing and her renovations and shopping for her sister's wedding. Luke can't stand being around Charlie when she's on one of her weird, anxious highs. Can't stand how her babbling snowballs with the radio's blare. Whenever she leaves the kitchen, he flicks the blasted thing off, though he knows she'll immediately yell out from wherever she is in the café, 'Hey, Luke, leave that *on* man!' Today he turns the radio off when she goes out for a smoko. After a few minutes of peace, she returns, dumps a pile of eggplants onto the stainless steel bench, flicks the radio back on and starts chopping.

And it begins. 'Fucking men,' she mutters. This is her usual reply to the news report. 'Fucking men.' Luke feels Dave bristle. Charlie carries on, oblivious as usual to Dave's anger. Luke tries to ignore the spiking atmosphere but can't help wondering, as he always does, why he isn't angry too. As Dave's fury pulses into the kitchen, Luke realises that he *is* bristling, but his anger is different. It's inside him, and blighted by confusion—for he agrees with her. 'Fucking men,' Charlie says. Fucking men, Luke repeats, inside. 'Fucking men,' she says. Fucking men, he replies, hating them, hating men, thinking, It *is* fucking men fucking everything up for most people most of the fucking time. On he works, horrified he has anything in common with Charlie's screwed-up head and horrified—more so—by the substance of what unites them. He suddenly feels claustrophobic. Tries to rein his panic in, but his mind races ahead. I'm a man, aren't I? How can I hate men? And if

239

I do, what the hell does *that* mean?

Luke carries on, as if these questions might dissolve under the pressure of his work. They don't. The news blasts on and on. A murder–suicide out west. Fucking men. Another bombing in Syria. Fucking men. A spate of acid attacks in Pakistan. *Fucking* men!

All the while, Dave's fury seeps into the kitchen. When the radio reports that a woman in Hobart has prostituted her nine-year-old daughter Dave goes straight for Charlie's throat. 'Fucking women!' he yells. *'Fucking women!'*

Luke freezes. His instinct is to grab Charlie: he's seen her fight on TV, when she won the state finals, and they've all seen her go nuts in the kitchen. Somehow, he holds steady. Keeps his head averted. Continues prepping, each of his senses straining to read the situation.

He hears Charlie stop slicing her eggplants. Feels her turn towards Dave. Sidelong, sees her knife held loose in her hand. Senses them face each other down. Feels her realise—perhaps for the first time ever—that her 'fucking men' spiel has sounded outside of her head. Into a room full of men. Forever, the dull heartbeat of Luke's chopping. The clink and clatter of the old dishie. The muted chatter of the café. Suddenly the room heaves as Charlie's anger rears up in her. Luke sees her tiny brown hand re-grip the knife. Sees that arm shake with tension. Listens to her low, jaw-clenched voice say, 'It's not *women* fucking the kid. It's not *women*, who want to fuck fucking *children*.' Senses her raise her knife.

Senses her gesture with it, slicing the air. Luke glances up then. He has to see what's happening. Has to assess what might happen.

Dave's face is white. Pearled with sweat. Frozen and freezing. Again, Luke sees who Dave is to his girl, his friends, his family. To himself. Not just a dreamy, awkward kid, but a kid who desperately wants to be a man. Luke watches as Dave refuses to submit. Refuses to let Charlie tell him that he is doomed because all men are doomed—doomed always to be men. '*I* don't want to fuck kids,' Dave says. He steps closer to her. Luke watches the tip of Charlie's knife press lightly into the starched white front of Dave's apron. Realises that Dave is also armed. '*I don't want to fuck kids,*' Dave repeats. He takes another step closer. Luke watches Charlie's knife slide up and along the fabric, till the length of its blade rests gently against the white, its tip pointed at Dave's chin. Luke realises that she has loosened her grip.

Suddenly Dave smashes his cleaver onto the steel bench. Everyone jumps. Charlie's knife thuds onto the rubber matting. Luke forces himself to return to his prepping. He glances up every couple of seconds, monitoring them as he tries to work out what to do. Dave suddenly directs his chilling voice at him. '*Luke* doesn't want to fuck kids, do you, Luke?' Luke only hesitates for a second. He hears the old alco stop in his dishwashing. Meets the dishie's amused gaze. Turns back to his chopping board. Carries on. Says nothing. The silence stretches, excruciating.

Finally, Luke senses Dave step back from Charlie. When Dave speaks again it is in his usual voice. 'And I'll be a *great* dad!' he says randomly, suddenly embarrassed. Then he stumbles to the door. Pauses. Turns around. 'We're not *all* pigs!' The quiver in his voice jerks Luke's face up again. He looks across the kitchen. Sees a boy veering between anger and tears—unsure if he's throwing a final punch or asking a question.

Luke returns to his work. Listens to Dave disappear out the back. Hears Charlie breathe again. Listens to her hurry into the cool room. Hears her return empty-handed. Thanks Christ for the distraction of the lunchtime rush.

As Miriam and Sarah appear and disappear at the servery window, they each notice that something is wrong, for though Charlie works with her usual manic efficiency, her fingers keep flicking up to her eyes. Miriam frowns an accusation at Luke. He shrugs. Sees her register Dave's absence. When the rush eases, Miriam returns with coffees for them. Silently squeezes Charlie's shoulder. Disappears out the back with a milkshake. As they finish up the final orders, Luke hears Charlie mumbling. In a low flat voice, she mutters, 'Every night.' She says it again, 'Every night. Every fucking night.'

Luke senses her stop in her work. Feels her pull herself up, as if realising, once again, that her thoughts are sounding outside of her head. Feels her look at him. Senses her desire, her need for him to look back at her, to answer her, to show her that he's heard her.

He ignores her. Keeps working.

Finally, she takes her coffee and cigarettes out the back to fix things up with Dave. Luke carries on alone then, finishing the few remaining orders while their words war inside him.

Fucking men.

Fucking women.

Fucking men.

Fucking women.

Fucking men fucking women.

Fucking men and fucking women fucking everything up for everyone forever.

Ø

Luke was thrown awake last night. Didn't know if he'd screamed out loud or in his head. Seconds of confusion as his face and hand seared. That old terror assailing him. That queer, banal terror, as real as hell and yet trained and contained by his brain's immediate and well-practised reply: It's not real, it's okay, it's just the skin dreaming. He lay awake for hours after that. At dawn, he stopped trying to sleep, got up, got dressed and walked down to the quarry. The black dog met him at the gate, as if she'd been waiting for him. Together, they walked down to his bench and watched the sky ease open above the lake. Now they are walking loops in the damp morning light. The dog trots ahead of him. Every minute or so, she stops and turns and waits, looking back as if to check he's following her. And he is. Headsore with sleeplessness, he's letting her lead the way.

It's another dreaded Sunday. As Luke wanders, he realises it's probably this fact that kept him awake last night. He's used to night terrors, but he'll never get used to these time-warping days off. At the restaurant he'd work fourteen-, fifteen-, even sixteen-hour shifts, seven days a week. He didn't want days off, and he wasn't offered them. So why, suddenly, had he thought those hours were doing him harm? Why did he think a crappy day job at a crappy café would be better? Normal hours. Normal life. Naïve idiot. All normal hours have done for him is rub his abnormality in his face. At the restaurant he lived at night. Now he understands why that mattered: night sits more gently on him than these endless cool-lit Sundays ever will.

The dog trots across the rock wall ahead of him. She stops halfway, turns around, waits. He picks over the boulders, taking his time. He wonders what Dave is doing right now. Sunday morning, he'll be in bed with his new girl in their new rental on the other side of the highway. They'll be looking forward to breakfast and papers and a long lazy day of nothing more than each other. A long day of nothing—of everything. Sunday. A day made for couples. For families. Sunday. A gaping black hole. A crushing torment that Luke is sure he'll never get a handle on. He wonders if Charlie is in bed with that pig of hers. Wonders if the pig is wanting it and taking it right now. Wonders what Miriam is doing in her unit. Does she have someone? He doubts it. Wonders if Jamie is staying with her this weekend or if he's away with his friends, or his dad, whoever that is. Maybe Jamie has a girl too. Luke tries to picture Sarah. Imagines her lying asleep in some man's arms, for surely she must be. Wonders what kind of a guy he is. Not, Luke thinks, a guy like me. A young guy. Good-looking. Smart. Funny. Kind. Knows what he's doing. Knows what to do. Isn't fucked up. Isn't going to fuck *her* up.

Luke steps over the granite, trying to imagine waking up next to Sarah on a Sunday morning. He can't. He can imagine fucking her brains out. He does. All the time. And the more he tries not to, the more he does it. He can imagine doing a thousand sick things to her, things he couldn't do in real life, even if he wanted to. But he can't imagine kissing her. Can't imagine being kissed by her. Can't imagine just being with her. On a couch. Watching TV. Eating dinner. Driving somewhere. Walking through a supermarket and arguing about things that don't matter, like which cereal or coffee or milk to buy. He can't imagine doing any of these things that so many people do so naturally every single day.

God, how he hates them! These idiots who just go about their lives, casual as can be, clueless as to what they've got. So many of them complaining, shitting all over everything they have, tearing each other to pieces for no good reason at all. Why? Don't they see it, the randomness, the sheer miracle of their lives together?

Luke tries to imagine lying in the darkness of his bedroom with Sarah. Tries to feel her skin on his skin. Her breath in his breath. But he can't, he can't. His memory of her face and body and smell and voice slip from him as soon as he tries to clutch her and pull her close.

Luke looks ahead at the dog. She is poised in the middle of the lake, gazing at him. Her tail swings its usual slow hello. When he reaches her, he sits next to her and it's like this, side by side, that they watch the night-glitter of the refinery fade into the rising day.

Ø

Luke heads for the office. He's early, but he's hurrying. He wants to get to the quarry before dark. He grabs his jacket, turns to go, and there she is, standing in the doorway with her arms crossed. Sarah. Bloody Sarah. She looks strange. Intense. Shy and wicked all at once. She smiles. Knows she's cornered him. Has cornered him on purpose. His gut clenches as her weird eyes laugh and hold him right where he is. She doesn't ask him to come to her gig. She *tells* him to. She's already written down the details. Does she know he can't refuse her? He mutters something about having plans, but he's taking the scrawled napkin from her. She nods, smiles, steps aside, releases him. As he passes her in the doorway he feels it: the radiant warmth of her skin meeting his.

He drives straight to the quarry. He has hours to fill before her show begins. As he drives, he's stunned by what washes through him. There's the dread he expects. A dread as real as the napkin shoved into his pocket. But there's something else. Something alien. Excitement. Hope. In the tiny office, under those brutal white lights, he'd seen that Sarah wanted him to come to her gig. That behind her smile was her anxiety—*her* anxiety—that he'd say no. He saw that she felt she was taking a risk. Saw that, to her, he was worth taking a risk for. Luke drives and recites the fact of it: Sarah wants me to come to her gig; Sarah wants me to come to her gig; *Sarah* wants *me*.

At the quarry, Luke hardly notices when the black dog appears and jumps her hellos at him. She nose-butts his empty hands and pockets, then trots ahead of him. Together they stride their usual rounds. Luke half-heartedly argues with himself about whether or not he should go, but by the time he reaches the gate he's stopped his pretence. Of course he'll go. He has to. Just this once, he tells himself, just in case. In case *what*? He doesn't dare put words to his hope. To his fear. Instead, he drives home. Showers. Puts on clean clothes. Avoids the mirror. Leaves for the station.

When he steps into the busy carriage, his excitement and hope immediately morph into a pure and perfect terror. The doors close behind him. Too late. He puts his head down. Shoves his bad hand into his pocket. Finds an empty seat in the middle of the carriage. He stares at the floor, counts the minutes and tries not to notice as, one by one, the people closest to him get up and move away. He tries to ignore what's happening. He can't: he's in a hall of mirrors. The train's night-black windows multiply his image all around him: a huge deformed man, circled by a moat of empty seats on a busy train. How can he have forgotten? The terrible sight of him. The immutable horrible fact of him. His image. His prison. Has it really been so long since he's been out? That old hurt and anger trickles through him, dammed only by the darkest parts of him that laugh and laugh at the absurdity of the scene. All these strangers, scared of *him*? They have no idea how terrified *he* is. Terrified of them, and by the very thing that they, at least, can walk away from.

When Luke finally makes it to the city, he keeps getting lost. Sarah's directions don't help. Everything has changed. Whole buildings are missing. Whole buildings have appeared. The streets seem to have moved. To have grown wider. Or narrower. Some even seem to have disappeared. He eventually finds the bar. It's at the end of a laneway full of garbage. He hesitates at the heavy wooden door. He double-checks her directions. He can't believe she's going to introduce her voice to the world in such a dump. But that's not why he's paralysed. He simply doesn't want to be here anymore. Not after that train ride. Not now that his excitement and hope have disappeared on him. Luke stares at the closed door, unable to act in any direction at all. He doesn't want to be here. Doesn't want to go home. Doesn't want to be anywhere. He turns to leave, but before he can, an army of very loud, very drunk and very jolly middle-aged women stampede down the alley towards him. One of them yells at him to get his big arse outa the way. The others laugh and shove him inside.

The bar is large, low lit and busy. No-one notices him. He moves through the crowd. He spots a tiny platform in the corner of the room. It's empty. As his eyes adjust to the dark he sees Sarah rummaging in the curtained shadows. He stops. She moves so that the single bulb above the stage lights her up, exaggerating her every feature. Her skin is too white. Her cheekbones too large. Her brows too thick and black. She looks more severe than usual—and stranger than ever. The only thing that softens her image is her hair. It hangs loose around her face, shimmering halfway down her waist. It's much longer than he's ever imagined it, and he's imagined it often. Imagined unclasping it from its tight daily knot. Imagined it tumbling over her sharp collarbones and her small white breasts. Her arms and legs and feet are bare. She wears a loose black dress gathered in a straight line above her chest like a child's. She looks like something from a magazine. From a movie. A fairy tale. She looks like a model. Like a kid.

He feels sick. Humiliated. Devastated. All at once he sees the sheer stupidity of his hopes. This Sarah is beyond him. Above him. Nothing like the girl he works with by day and fantasises about at night. When this hits him, he turns and makes for the door. Too slow. Miriam materialises by his side. 'Luke!' she says. 'You came!' She grabs his gnarled arm and drags him back to the bar. Baffled and suddenly exhausted, he submits.

He lets her lead him, his mind slowly registering just how different *she* seems. Her frizzy curls have somehow straightened into a burnt-orange cascade that pours over her bare shoulders. She wears a tight, sparkly dress that is completely unlike the baggy T-shirts and jeans she submerges herself in at the café. He watches her plump little body as she struts ahead of him on her stocky legs. So fleshy. So twinkly. So energetic. So *different*.

Miriam plonks him on a seat next to her at the bar. As she looks for Sarah—who seems to have disappeared—Luke studies her. He's so used to evading her evasiveness, so used to damning her face's ugly tear-puffed misery, that he's never looked at her properly. Covertly, he watches her turn and order them drinks. Sees that it isn't just her appearance that's different. Not just her dress and her hair and the way she's made up her face. There's something inside her—something he's never seen before—that's shining right into the room. He watches her laugh and flirt with the barman. Notices the barman laugh and flirt with her. Watches her turn and smile as she hands him his beer. Meets her raised glass with his own. Watches her swivel to face the stage, her elbows propping her up on the bar. Feels how every part of her is open to this room, to its people, to the night, to him. She can't stop smiling! For a second, Luke forgets the sickening slap of Sarah's other-worldliness. For a second, he's returning Miriam's irresistible smile as the first warm flush of his drink washes through him. But only for a second. On the tail end of that chemical rush comes a flood of confusion.

What the hell is going on? Who is who? Which version of these women is real? And what about him? With a shock he realises he likes being seen at a bar with a woman. Is that it? That he likes being seen with a woman? Or that he likes being seen with Miriam? Even as Luke savours this pleasure he tastes its taint. Miriam is different in this place. Sarah has transformed too. Has he? Or is he merely a thousand times more himself—a thousand times more freakish—next to their glittering strangeness?

Sarah finally reappears. She steps onto the stage. Luke feels her fear spin out across the room. It silences everyone. The crowd stare up at her. He senses them judge her unusual and extreme beauty. Feels them poised, ready to judge her voice. He is shocked by their hostility. By how her fear seems to feed it. He feels Miriam next to him, willing Sarah to move, just as he is. Willing her to begin, to flee, to do something—to do anything. As Sarah's mute terror fills the room, he is struck again by how much he's overestimated her age. She really does look like a teenager. A kid. And maybe, he thinks, that's all she is. Worse, he realises, it's not that he's overestimated her age, but that he's underestimated his own. There is Sarah, as vulnerable as a child. And here he is, realising for the first time that he is well and truly middle-aged. Old enough to be her father. He recoils, but nothing can stop Dave's pained cries resounding across the silent, judging bar. *I don't*

251

want to fuck kids, Charlie! *Luke* doesn't want to fuck kids, do you, Luke? Luke cowers into his beer. Dave had begged him for affirmation. Dave had needed truth as affirmation, but the most honest answer Luke could give him was silence. And, as Luke stares up at Sarah, that alien and beautiful girl-woman on the stage, he still cannot answer. Or will not. So he tries to forget Dave and Charlie. Tries to focus on willing Sarah's fear away for her.

When it gets too hard to look at her, Luke turns to Miriam instead. But there is no relief there. Free from the fear and worry she bears around the café, he sees that she too is a good deal younger than he is. With a stab of something sharp and bitter—Pity? Anger? And if it's anger, anger at whom?—he realises she must have had Jamie when she was just a kid herself. Why hasn't he realised this before? Where has he been this past year at the café? Where has he been these past two decades? *Two decades.*

Abruptly, Sarah stops staring. She adjusts the microphone. She sits down and strums a couple of chords. Luke feels another wave of expectation surge towards her, palpable, terrifying. She doesn't look up. Doesn't introduce herself. She just crosses one leg over the other, positions her guitar across her knee and begins to play. She taps a slow rhythm with her foot and begins to sing in her low, husky voice. The quiet talk resumes, faltering to silence each time Sarah's voice rises, higher and clearer than Luke has ever heard it at the café. It's horrible to listen to. Excruciating. These are songs he's never heard before. As he listens he realises these songs are her own. No. Worse. These tragic songs *are her.*

On he drinks. Tries to blind and deafen himself to her nakedness. Why is she doing this to herself? To everyone else? Why is she doing this to *him*? He remembers the first time the black dog let him pat her. How she'd collapsed to the ground, belly up, limbs loose, offering herself to him in total trusting submission. Stupid dog. Stupid Sarah. Luke drinks and looks everywhere except at the stage. He half watches Miriam beside him. Glimpses the faces around them. Sees his embarrassment and pain multiplied across the room. Recognises the crowd's flinch-frozen posture. Sees how everyone is again transfixed by Sarah as she tells them everything that has ever happened to her. Everything they had never known. Nothing, nothing anyone could *ever* have imagined.

Sarah keeps singing. Luke keeps drinking. Soon, the people around him begin to pitch and sway. He tries to focus on the floor, but people's shoes and legs blur around him, coming close, moving back. There, a pair of men's legs, ugly in tight patterned jeans. Luke wants to punch him. There, a pair of women's feet in strappy shoes, toenails as shiny and black as beetles. Disgusting. Teeth gleam in red mouths, eyes roll in sweaty faces, hands shape up the air.

And then, two bandaged, sandalled feet. It's Quang. Shy and smiling, he's turned up with three beers. He gives one to Luke and then shuffles over to sit on the other side of Miriam. They sit there together, three in a row, listening to Sarah strip herself bare. As they watch her, she looks up for the first time. Luke sees her notice Quang. Sees—no, feels—their eyes lock. She gives Quang the slightest nod and smile. That smile. How it springs to her lips: she can't help it, and it re-shapes her voice so that her words stop ripping out of her and instead begin to arc up, up and away from her. The whole room ripples as her smile-shaped voice begins to tell a different story from its own words. Drunkenly, stupidly, Luke makes the connection. Quang is Sarah's guy. Sarah is Quang's girl. How did *that* happen? When did that happen?

Luke remembers Sarah's mute rage when Miriam refused to call Quang an ambulance. Who was Sarah angry at then? He remembers her taking the envelope from Miriam the next day. Was that the beginning of it? Or had Sarah and Quang led their secret life togeth-er for longer? Sarah and Quang. It doesn't sound right. He repeats it to himself. Sarah and Quang. Quang and Sarah. It will never sound right to him, but as he watches their eyes meet across the dim-lit bar, he knows that, to each other, they are the rightest, truest thing in the world. Just like the photo of Dave's girlfriend, Sarah and Quang's locked eyes make Luke glimpse that world—that home—that so many people build for each other, out of each other. A world as whole and separate and im-penetrable as the one he's built for himself. All that stuff in his head—his stupid adolescent hopes, his fucked-up fantasies, his moronic belief that Sarah would ever want *him*—that's the wrong thing. Luke and Sarah? Luke and anyone? *He* is the wrong thing, again, still, always.

After Quang's arrival everything speeds up, disconnects. There's a stop-gapped image of Miriam and Quang laughing, trying to dance around his mummified feet. A flash of Miriam's waterfall of red hair, rippling with her movement under the orange lights. A close-up of Sarah next to him at the bar. Big eyed. Flushed faced. Asking him without asking him what he thinks of her songs. What does he say? He mumbles something. She doesn't understand. He raises his bottle to her. Salutes her but can barely meet her blazing eyes after all that she's exposed and, especially, after seeing her as Quang's, Quang as hers. There's Quang and Sarah dancing together on a half-empty dance floor. They move slowly, pressed close except where they tiptoe around his wounded feet.

And there's his own slow panic, slugging through him. He's drunk too much. He can't stop drinking. He tries to stand. Sits straight back down. It isn't just his liquid legs that have him reeling. It's how unreal everyone looks. Intensified. Their faces and their bodies. Their lines and their limbs. Their lights and their darks. Everything exaggerated. Grotesque. Beautiful. He spins and sits. Sits and keeps spinning. Watches them all and tries to work out what is real and what is not. He feels as if he is seeing everyone for the first time. Feels this and wonders again if they see him anew. And if they do, does he seem more like them outside of the café's white-lit kitchen? Or even more monstrous? His body answers him, needling his scars with the sixth-sense knowledge that, while he is watching them, for once no-one is watching him. Relief at that. Relief, and an ache of grief.

Later, when Sarah and Miriam dance together on the empty floor, Luke tries to stand again. Looks at his feet. Watches his shoes move everywhere, go nowhere. Is he dancing too? He feels the urge to laugh. No, no, it's not laughter. It's the drink heaving in him. Chokes it back. He's out in the lane. Feels the ground rush at him. Something smacks into his head. The stink of rotting rubbish. He's walking. Hot in his face. Cold in his body. A crowd of laughing girls. Sudden silence. They scatter around him like colourful birds. He walks on. Bare legs everywhere, luminous against the bitumen. Legs and heels. Legs and heels. A group of guys hanging around a doorway. One yells at him. The others laugh. He keeps going. The neon glow of shop signs. The hard white rhythm of street lights. The red and white and amber flicker of cars coming and going along the city streets. Then the icy, dark silence of the suburbs. Wide empty streets. No footpaths. Cold. Walking. Cold. Walking. Cold. Blackness.

Then, one crisp, clear moment in the middle of the night. Luke opens his eyes. Sees the Milky Way. Doesn't know where he is. Is he at the farm? Doesn't know the time. Just looks up and thinks, Beautiful. Looks up and thinks, Sarah has no friends. We were the only people she knew at her first-ever show. The dark shivers. The Milky Way dips and slips above him. Wrapped in this one warm thought—I am Sarah's friend; I can love her too—Luke sinks back into his poisoned sleep.

Ø

Luke wakes up on his bench. He lies there, staring up at the glaring grey. It might be dawn. It might be dusk. He has no idea what day it is. When he tries to sit up, dizziness thrusts him down again. His brain crashes into his skull with every movement. He's numb with cold. Frozen, except for his hot and clammy face. Though sick and confused, he knows enough to damn himself for being so stupid. If his dad taught him anything, it was that drinking and sleeping out are as good a way as any to kill yourself. Is that why he's here? Was he meant to wake up? He rolls onto his side. Bile pours out of him onto the dirt. Hot and bitter. His whole body rails against whatever it is that he's done to it. He tries to sit up again. He puts his head between his knees. Waits for the shocks of nausea to take on a regular beat. Makes himself stand. The lake and its granite belt stagger and swing. He waits. Breathes. Studies the biggest rock in the middle of the wall until his vertigo passes. Then he heads off on his usual loop.

Did he *walk* here? He can't remember catching the train home. But he also can't remember the hours it would have taken him to walk from the city. Can't remember entering the quarry. Does remember, finally and only, waking to that singular moment in the depths of the night. I am Sarah's friend. As he circles the lake, the sky begins to merge from silver to white. He's relieved it's early and not late. Relieved that the daytime hasn't witnessed whatever mess got him here in the first place. He keeps walking. Lets the air cool his burning face. Lets his arms and legs swing warmth back into his frozen core. As his nausea begins to ease, images of last night begin to replay in his mind. That's it. He was out with people. He was drinking at a bar. He was doing what normal people do on a Friday night. And if yesterday was Friday, today is Saturday. With a weary, sickening pang he remembers Charlie has her sister's wedding today. That he has to be at the café in an hour or so, getting the place ready for breakfast. That he'll have to manage Dave on their busiest morning of the week. Luke ups his stride, hoping his pace will thin the muck in his blood before he arrives at the café.

By the time he comes to the clearing where the road meets the lake, his nausea is shifting. He stops. Surveys the crushed cans and plastic bags scattered everywhere. He tries to remember how many weeks since he last saw the kids here. Two? Three? There are fresh tyre marks grooved into the mud, crisscrossing older marks that have been fossilised by the frost. He walks over to the dead campfire. Squats next to it. Pokes one of its charred logs. Even though the fire is cold, his hands hover above it, palms down. He closes his eyes and lets the dawn blast of the birds and the crisp and creak of the gums soothe his drumming head.

It's crouched like this that Luke suddenly feels her. He opens his eyes. Looks around. Nothing. He clicks his dry and sour tongue, making that sharp sound she's come to respond to, the sound that stops her in her tracks so that she turns and gazes at him, her eyes bright and questioning. He listens for her. Clicks his tongue. Nothing. Slowly, he stands. Silently, he waits. He can feel her. He can feel her like she's his own skin.

Then he hears it. Barely distinguishable from the breeze that carries it, the faintest of cries.

Adrenaline ices his blood. His nausea and dizziness shoot away. He stands still, his skin stinging. Again, he hears her. He begins to trace the edge of the clearing. Stops every few paces to listen. To lean down. To peer into the scrubby undergrowth. He finds himself jogging, suddenly desperate to find her. Forces himself to slow down. Walk. Search properly. Listen harder. He's poised on the edge of panic. Another soft, whining cry. The breeze seems to carry her to him from every direction. On he goes, crouched over, searching. Moving and stopping. Clicking his tongue, begging for and dreading her reply.

He reaches the water's edge. As his feet sink into the tarry silt, he suddenly hears heavy gurgled breaths close to him.

She is there, lying on her side. She is half hidden under a waterlogged shrub. Her back legs are submerged in the cold·water. The front half of her body is on the bank, dry. Her head rests in the mud. The gurgling comes from within her. The eye that should look up at him—that clear amber eye—is closed. The eye that should look up at him, that should see him as it has always seen him, is swollen and shut and crusted with blood. He cannot tell if there is an eye there at all. Dizziness spins through him. Slowly, quietly, he steps closer to her. He doesn't want to see this. He can't bear to see this. Can't stand to hear that gurgled cry—and the only thing worse than hearing this sound, is recognising it. With every step he tries to remember how he ended up at the quarry last night. With every stomach-clenched reply to the bloody storm of her breathing, the words throb in his head. How did I get here last night? Why did I come here? Did I do this? *Did I do this?*

He stands over her. Torpor numbs him, just as it did when he was faced with Quang's boiling feet. He gazes down at the dog. She is dying. She has been lying here dying and crying for hours. She tries to tilt her lovely, ruined face up at him. She cannot lift her head. He feels the slick of mud pull at his feet. The mud is eating her, he thinks. There is mud on her other eye, stuck in her lids. He looks again at her waterlogged legs. At her submerged tail uncurled on the bed of the lake.

He stares at that silent tail.

Then, he is kneeling in the water next to her. He hears his voice making soft, low noises. Sees his disgusting hand offer itself to her nose, his skin telling her, It's me, it's just me. His skin begging her to answer the terrible questions exploding inside him. The dog sniffs the air between her nose and his skin. She shudders. Another gurgled gasp. He cannot read her. Her body no longer talks. She does not move as he strokes his hand across her lean satin lengths, looking for where she hurts. The low sounds keep rolling from his mouth, as foreign to him as Sarah's voice last night. His hands search gently for the hurt. The black dog continues to cry in the same choked rhythm. She hurts everywhere, everywhere. Even though his mind recoils from her agony and from itself—not knowing what to do; not knowing what he's done—his body is calm. His hands move into the freezing water. His fingers slide into the slime beneath her. She does not struggle. With one swift and strong movement he heaves her up from the suck of mud. He braces against the thought of her pain. She gasps and gurgles, gasps and gurgles. Slowly, holding her firm and close to his broad chest, Luke begins to walk.

He feels one of the black dog's lean and muscled legs—one of the legs that made her fly—swing like a pendulum as he walks. A dead leg. Did I do this? Hears the hot bubble of her breath. Her lungs filling with blood. Did I do this? Looks at her velvet face pressed into his chest. Except for where it crusts with blood, it is the softest, blackest little face he has ever known. He looks over her ridiculous ears at the eye that lay in the silt. It is muddied but open and whole. Her lid flutters. Her eye wanders lazily. Looks everywhere. Looks nowhere. Did I do this? He walks on along the dirt path. Looks out across the lake. Listens as her breaths come fewer and further between, hurting her, drowning her. Hugs her. Pulls her closer to his chest as if his lungs can breathe for her. Grips her with his good and bad arms. Grips her tighter and tighter. Embraces her, like this, till she is quiet. Still. Stopped. Safe.

Finally, he reaches his bench. He sits. Carefully arranges her on his lap. Makes a warm cave for her with his chest and shoulders and arms and bent head. Presses his face into her icy wet neck. Breathes her. Damp fur and soil and silt and leaf litter. The lake, the quarry, the sky, the dirt, the refinery. Breathes all of her, all of her.

For a long time, Luke sits in the dawn, clutching the soft and sodden weight of the black dog's beautiful mongrel body. He cannot let her go. He cannot stop crying. And he cannot stop the words roaring through him: Did I do this? Did I do this? Did I do this?

Ø

Luke can hardly remember burying the black dog at the quarry. Knows only that he laid her somewhere near the lake, near the bench where he first saw her. He remembers feeling cold as he walked away. Remembers how, when he got home, he went straight to the phone and called the café. It must have been about lunchtime. He knew Dave would be panicking. Knew it wasn't fair to leave him to manage the Saturday rush alone. But he didn't care. He rang and, as soon as the phone picked up, said, 'It's Luke. I'm not coming in.' He hung up before anyone could reply. Then he went and sat in his living room. Wet and muddy and bloody, he sat there feeling nothing other than a mild anger each time the phone rang. It rang all day. He assumed it was Miriam. She didn't give up until late in the afternoon.

When the static grey silence of dusk filled the unit, Luke finally stood. He walked outside to his tiny grassed yard. He undressed. Dumped his stain-hardened clothes in the bin. Went back inside, to the bathroom. Showered. Got into bed. Fell asleep immediately. Slept until late the next morning. Woke. Slowly realised it was Sunday. Showered again and found himself walking to the quarry. He wandered its gravelled tracks all day. He turned sharply any time someone came in his direction. Had no direction himself. Was just walking that long, long day away. Didn't head for home till it was dark. Till he was dizzy with hunger and cold. When he got back to his unit, he showered again. Got into bed. Slept.

Now, it's been a week since the black dog died. Luke still wanders the cleaved lake morning and night: beginning loops without ending them; turning one way, then the other. A dozen times he crosses the rock wall. Closes his eyes. Begs the quarry's music to fill him and hold him upright like it used to. It doesn't. It won't. It can't, because of the four terrifying words that chain-react inside him, deafening him to everything else. Did I do it? Did I do it? Did I do it?

Perhaps he shouldn't come here anymore. This is her

place. Was her place. Not his, never his. Perhaps returning here, like this, will kill him too. For his body hasn't understood what's happened. It still listens for the paw-press and twig-snap of her playful stalking. Still longs for her to be there, trotting next to him, looking up at him. Trotting ahead of him, gazing back at him, waiting for him. Still searches for her gleam speeding through the shadows. It's just a dog, he tells himself. It's just a dog, just a dog. But every time he forgets and remembers that she's dead, every time he forgets and remembers how she died, he wants to walk himself into that flooded tip and sink himself forever. And it's not just her absence that draws him to the lake's ashen filth. It's his mind's unrelenting struggle against its own accusations. Did I do it? Of course I didn't. But I've done it before. I've done it before.

On the farm, they could justify killing anything they named a pest. Not that they justified anything back then. And nothing explains all the other stuff they did. Why did they do it? Because they could? No. It was more than that. It was worse than that. The fact was, it felt great. More exciting than busting up the dust around the dam in their cars. More gratifying than any time he'd ever spent with a girl. Was that it? He'd found something he was good at? Something he was the *best* at? Something he knew how to do? The hunt. The torture. The shot and slit and slap of the kill.

Luke continues his aimless rounds of the lake. Stares at the ghostly gums. Sees the masterpieces of his dog trees. They were stunning. Stark. Something like art. He remembers the excitement that stirred inside him as he drove towards them. As he watched the eerie fact of the dogs' dense bodies emerge from the long strips of bark that blew back and forth around them, as light as lace. On he walks. Remembers the one time he'd spotted the black dog before she spotted him. Sees her poised on the rock wall in the middle of the lake. Watches her pivot and fly along the boulders. The envy that flooded him then! How totally and completely she knew what she was made for. How she revelled in it. On he walks, bracing himself against these punches of memory and the terrible questions they drag with them. What am *I* made for? What have *I* revelled in?

For a week, he's walked the lake like this. For a week, he's damned and forgiven himself a thousand times. Told himself that, no matter what he's done in the past, no matter what he'd once loved to do, he'd stopped doing it. It had stopped exciting him, hadn't it? It had started to sicken him, hadn't it? What was it that changed everything? Was it his dad, surrendering to the dogs and the drink? Was it the fact that the dogs were winning? What *was* it about that brindle beast that threw him off the farm forever? When he jammed his heel into its face, that had been an act of mercy. Hadn't it? That was the least cruel thing he could do. Wasn't it? But whose torture was he ending?

For a week, Luke has stared into the black dog's single muddied eye as she tried to look up at him while she died in his arms. For a week, he has stared into the stoic gaze of the wild dog he'd crushed to silence so long ago. Perhaps that was it. That feral was the first animal whose eyes had locked onto his, looked at him, seen him, and demanded to be seen.

Ø

On Monday, Luke wakes with a start. It isn't yet light. His pillow is wet. He's disoriented. He searches his mind for echoes of the usual nightmares. Nothing. Realises it isn't a night sweat that's woken him. It's tears. Bloody tears. Furious, he throws himself out of bed. Goes to the quarry. Walks until it's time to go home and get ready for work. Drives to the café. Strides into the kitchen as if it's right and reasonable for him to disappear for a week and then reappear without explanation. Head down, he puts his apron on and returns to his usual spot between Charlie and Dave. Tries to act normal. Realises, quickly, that he isn't the only one acting. Everyone is tiptoeing around him. As the day wears on, he gets more and more nervous. What's going on? What do they know? Surely no-one could have seen him with the dog. Seen him carrying her. Seen him burying her. And all Miriam could have known is that he bailed on a week's work without notice or explanation. Yet everyone seems to sense that something has happened to him.

Miriam and Sarah hover over him all week. Their mute concern is suffocating. A dozen times Luke endures Dave's self-conscious, back-slapped hellos. Even Charlie sits on her tempers and her tantrums. By the end of the week, Luke is certain that something is going on. Forget the black dog. Perhaps he's about to get sacked for disappearing as he did. Or worse. Maybe something happened that night at the bar. That was the last time he'd seen them before everything changed. What the hell did he do that night?

Now it is Saturday. The café is packed. Luke is trying to quell his growing sense of portent by making eight breakfast bagels at once. He's so immersed in this, so desperate to immerse, that he's the last to notice when the cheerful buzz of the customers dips. It's Charlie and Dave who make him stop. They suddenly freeze in their work, listening, bracing.

Cane—storming through the café. What is he doing here? Something must have happened to him too. Something bad enough to send him home from overseas early, and in a blazing fury.

Seconds later Cane marches Miriam past the servery window. Cane's face is red and sweating. Miriam's is ashen, her eyes ugly and small. The office door slams shut. Charlie's and Dave's hands begin to stumble in time with the rise and fall of Cane's assault. Luke puts his head down and keeps working. Tries to ignore their panic. Tries to do the work they suddenly can't. Tries to avoid Sarah's bright-eyed anger as she runs from the kitchen to the café, managing the floor on her own. But the diatribe goes on and on, pouring into the hallway like sewage. Soon, even the customers grow quiet, and it's their silence—that shared, shocked silence—that finally makes Luke act.

He doesn't think or plan any of it. He simply feels the silence stop the movement of his mauled hand. Feels the silence remove the cool and heavy knife from his grip. Feels it walk him out of the kitchen and push his great weight against the putrid wake of Cane's words.

Luke doesn't hesitate at the office door. Doesn't knock. He simply opens it. Sees Miriam cowed into a corner. Feels his old and cruel anger towards her. Pathetic, he thinks. You stupid pathetic bitch. Sees Cane standing over her. Short and hard and pumped. Sees his fists shaking on their own clenched tension. Sees gobs of spit curdling at the corners of his mouth. Cane glares at him. His eyes—all pupil—spark madly. 'What do you fucking want, you fucking *freak*?' Luke just stands where he is, solid and tall and quiet. Wonders, vaguely, why he feels such disgust at Miriam but feels nothing at all for Cane. Watches Cane's face flare and wince, flushing and blanching as if his blood can't keep up with the tides of anger coursing through him. As Luke watches this, he suddenly understands. There is nothing on the planet that can stop Cane doing what he is doing. It's as if his frenzy and his foulness aren't coming from him, but happening to him.

As Luke realises this, he notices Cane's glazed eyes shift so that he is looking into the hallway. Luke feels Sarah behind him, her anger a wall of fire that awakens his own. Feels her body telling his that he isn't feeling nothing for Cane. He's just feeling something new. A different kind of rage. As pure and simple as any element. Free from the confusion of other emotions. From the contortions of being directed at any particular person. A brittle crystalline rage aimed at the whole blasted world. At all the thousands of things that happen to people. At all the inextricable threads that knot and warp and mat and tear at an animal's body and make what is happening in that office—in the kitchen, in the café, in the street, in his unit, on the farm, in the quarry, everywhere, *everywhere*—possible. Luke feels Sarah's identical feeling. And he feels her beg silently for the same thing that he is, that Miriam is, that Charlie and Dave and the rest of the damned café is. The same thing that Cane is begging for too. For it to stop, to stop, to *stop*.

Though registering Luke and Sarah's presence—their protest—Cane turns around and keeps screaming at Miriam. Luke steps into the office then. He steps right between them: his back towards Miriam; his chest facing Cane. But Cane keeps on at her. Just keeps on at her as if no-one else is there. When he calls her 'a dumb fucking cunt', Luke swiftly shoves him through the open door. Sarah jumps out of the way. Cane falls hard, cracks his head loudly on the hall tiles. Luke slams the office door shut. For a second, pure silence. Just him and Miriam, in the office, listening. Just the kitchen and the café and the rest of the world, listening. Then, the muffled torrent of Sarah's voice through the door, low and sharp and fast. A thump. And another. Moaning. Then the stomping fury of Cane as he stumbles down the hallway, kicking the skirting boards and bellowing. Luke listens to all of this with his back turned to Miriam. So what if she's crying? When isn't she crying? He waits until he hears the metallic crash of the back gate opening and bouncing shut again. Then he stares at the closed door for a while. Waits for the café's chat to resume, but when it finally does it is muted. Then he returns to the kitchen.

Though no-one looks up when he enters, the room is buzzing. Charlie can't keep the big fat smirk out of her voice as she bosses Dave about. She turns up the radio and begins her usual hyper-happy dance, bouncing around the kitchen. Dave hums along, massacring a cake that he isn't meant to be icing. Even the dishie whistles and nods at Luke as he resumes his place at the bench. Luke ignores them. He collects the backlog of dockets that Charlie and Dave have forgotten about. He ploughs through them alone and tries to feel what they feel. The victory of it. The justice of it. But he only feels sick.

What just happened? What has he seen? Luke tries to focus on his work. The buttery crisp of pastry. The vivid rainbow of a salad. The oily black silk of an olive. He tries to ignore the hopelessness tugging at him, but the harder he tries the more he feels the caverns inside him gape and billow, as huge and dark and empty as ever.

Ø

That afternoon, on her way out the door, Charlie stuns everyone by leaping up and smacking a kiss onto

Luke's ruined cheek. Then she just stands there, staring straight into his eyes, steady and unembarrassed and oblivious to the tragedy of her own face: her grin and childish glee; her cut lip and puffy, bruised eye; her makeup smeared everywhere, hiding nothing, exposing everything. Luke can barely return her gaze. Dave soon follows her out the door, grabbing Luke's bad hand and shaking it with both of his own, bashful as a kid. Once they're gone, Luke lingers in the kitchen. He's killing time. He isn't just waiting for Miriam to count the till and leave. He's putting off the new torment of his nights. Both his unit and the lake are intolerable to him now, and so he potters around the kitchen until long after the café is silent. Eventually, he wanders to the office to get his things.

And there she is. Miriam hasn't gone home at all. Instead, she's sitting there, tucked into her jacket with her bag on her lap. Her tears and her smiles fight their usual war across her face as she looks up at him. He stumbles back. She stands, no doubt remembering the last time he fled from her. She stops him with his name. 'Luke?' she says. 'Luke?' Torpid, he nods at her. Stares at her mouth as she repeats his name. 'Luke?' She is caught on his name, his name as a question. Panic flares inside him. What is this? Again, he wants to hit her. What does he care what her damn problems are? What does he care about her, or Cane, or any of them? He only wanted to make Cane shut up. Only wanted to stop Cane ruining the one thing that he, Luke, was good at. Making food. Making good food. Finally Miriam stops repeating his name. She pulls herself up to her full height. He refuses to meet her eye. Stares, instead, over her shoulder. 'The thing is, Luke …' Her voice trails off. She takes a deep breath. Irritation ripples through him. When she finally speaks again, her voice drifts up from a cooler, drier place than her tears. Luke hears this shift. Feels it. Suddenly knows that whatever it is she is about to say *he doesn't want to hear it*. She locks him again with his name and her eyes. She says, 'The thing is, Luke, he's his dad.'

Luke realises he is shaking his head. That he looks like he is gesturing incomprehension. That he doesn't understand. Can't understand. Won't.

She keeps her eyes fixed on his. Keeps her tear-ruddy face set. 'Luke,' she says. 'Cane's Jamie's dad.'

Ø

Only now, hours later, as he sits on the rock wall with the clear night sky sparkling above him, does Luke see it. It was pride that hammered her soft, round features into stone. It was pride that stared him down. That dared him to ignore or deny what she had to say. Three tiny words. Cane's. Jamie's. Dad. Words that Luke didn't want to hear. Words that she recoiled from even as she spoke them. But though she flinched, she refused to turn away. Her eyes shone. Grasped at him. Forced him to look back at her and see all the mess and struggle that was her life. He did as she wanted. He looked.

He saw. And when she quietly asked him not to tell anyone because nobody knew, except Cane, he nodded. And when her defiant, desperate eyes held him as she explained that she just wanted him to know how things were, he nodded again.

Luke stares across the water and wonders if any of it really happened. So strange. And incredible, that he did not hesitate: even as a part of him froze—both for and at her, cruelly repelled—he walked straight into the office. It had felt like déjà vu, as if a long-forgotten memory had re-awoken inside him. Something deeper than his scars. Something both of and older than himself. Something built into his very DNA. Whatever it was, it heard her, and it knew to move him straight to her. It knew to make him grab her and pull her roughly into his arms. It knew to press her close to him. To wrap her in his body—just as he had the black dog—as if his blood and bone could somehow shield her from the irrevocable facts of her life.

Luke hugs his knees. Guards himself from the cold black air. And he damns himself. For his stupidity. For his years of fear. Avoidance. Anger. Because it was unlike anything he could ever have imagined. There was nothing humiliating in it. Nothing fucked up, nothing sordid about it. It was its own thing. It wasn't just his scars, but hers. Not just his fears, his loneliness, his hopes and needs and screwed-up past, but *hers too*, hers too. Not just the terrible things he's done and had done to him, but her whole life's worth of struggle laid bare.

As Miriam had burrowed into him he felt his life-time of thinking and feeling heave up inside him—something whole and huge and brittle. Felt it buckle and break. Felt something new form. Something that sliced and shimmered—like water, like light—making his core roar out in sorrow and joy, You idiot! You fool! It's not what you think that matters, it's what you *do*. Hold her. Hold her. Hold her.

Ø

It's only when he hears their cars across the lake that he realises he's been pacing. A wolf in a cage, waiting. Waiting, and trying to work things out.

There's the shock and joy of discovering Miriam. The terror of knowing things can be different. The torment of his stop-gapped memory from that drunken night, when he woke and found the dying dog. How did he get from the city to the quarry? There's the image of the kids fighting and fucking around the fire, weeks before then. The memory of the black dog next to him, watching them. He's tried to imagine her entering the clearing after he ran away. Wondered if she already knew them. And why not? They had food too. And warmth. He pictures her jutting ribs. Her thin satin fur. Her bald belly. She was only trying to survive like anyone else. And maybe he'd gotten her used to people. Gotten her to trust people. But why would they hurt her? Luke sees the brindle dog, gasping and staring and asking him the same question. No answer then. No answer now. That's why he'd left the farm. There were too many questions and not enough answers out there.

Luke hears their cars screech to a stop. He begins to jog towards the clearing. He has no idea what he's doing, but he's already pumped with adrenaline. He must find out for certain that he didn't hurt her. (I couldn't have. But I've done it before. How can I be so sure? *And what do I do if it was me?*) He can make out some of their words as he draws closer. Fuck. Cunt. Fuck. Cunt. Laughter. Hears music playing from their cars. Slows down when he sees the glow of their fire. Keeps to the edge of the track till he's standing where he and the black dog once stood together. It could be the same scene. Despite the late-winter freeze, the kite-surfing girl is swinging her long bare legs off the end of the ute. Like last time, she is tucked into the arm of her guy. There's three kids around the fire tonight. Two of them are huddled together, talking. The third sits by himself, poking the fire with a stick, his face hidden under his hood. The others mill around, talking and joking, swearing and laughing. Luke suddenly isn't sure—as he wasn't with Sarah—just how old they are. Just how old *he* is. He stands in the shadows and watches the fire warp their pale, laughing faces. Remembers the rocks he rolled over the black dog's grave, as if it weren't too late to stop the world from getting at her.

Luke watches from the dark. He can hardly believe it when the girl and guy begin to muck around exactly as they did before. Again, she grabs at him. Again, he hits her back, returns to her. Again, Luke can't look away from their ritual—for he sees, now, that it is a ritual. So violent. So public. Why? Who are they doing this for? As the couple begin to kiss and grope, the others wolf-whistle and scatter, just as before. Luke sees now what he didn't see then. Their embarrassment. Their anger submerged into jokes and bluster. How could he have missed the mix of rage and envy in their ar-se-humping carry-on? He watches them as they begin to tease the kids by the fire. Realises they're not bullying. They're just desperate for distraction. Tonight, nobody is hauled into a wrestle. After a few kicks and head cuffs, the boys and men just sit and squat and stand around the fire, staring at its lashing flames, waiting for it all to be over.

Why do they stay? If they hate it, why do they stay? Luke looks at the couple in the ute. How, he wonders, can two people rule over so many so easily?

Luke steps towards the group. At first no-one notices him. The fire only intensifies the darkness of the shadows. Now he is the black dog. A patch of black in the blackness. A shadow stalking light. For a second he wavers. He still has time to turn. He still has time to leave without anyone noticing.

He steps forwards: he needs to know.

He steps into the circle of light, the circle of men: he must know.

The fire flares behind him. He pulls himself up. Pushes his shoulders back, his arms relaxed by his side.

He will *not* look down and away tonight. He will *not* press his ruined arm in, close to his body, out of sight. Not tonight, not tonight. Let them be scared, disgusted, horrified. Let them see a freak—a monster—and let them be terrified.

He walks straight past the silent group. Walks to the ute.

The guy and the girl are the last to realise that something has shifted around them. As the others' silence seeps into the clearing, they suddenly stop. 'What the *fuck*?' the man says, glancing at Luke and then over Luke's shoulder at the men and boys around the fire. The girl pulls away, tugs down her skirt, scuttles to the back of the tray. She crouches there, her arms crossed in front of her, as if she's about to get hit. And maybe you are, Luke thinks. Maybe you are.

The man in the ute scowls. Struggles to do up his pants. Keeps glancing at the others. Luke senses their paralysis. Feels their fear swell through him like a transfusion. He looks at the kitesurfer. Sees her lips tremble. Sees her recognise him. What was it he'd said to her that day on the path? 'It's not safe. It's not safe.' Luke sees she is shaking. Stupefied with fear. Because of me, he thinks, because of *me*. Excitement floods through him, delicious. He takes that electric surge and directs it at the thug in front of him. Stares down and waits for something to happen.

Suddenly, the man jumps off the tray so they're standing chest to chest. He's more than a head shorter, and probably half Luke's weight. Though he stands tall and squared and ready, his eyes keep darting over Luke's shoulder. No-one moves. Fear quivers across the man's face. When Luke recognises this—the child in the man—he wants to destroy him. Instead, in a calm, low voice, he asks, 'Have you seen a dog?'

The words ripple around the clearing.

Something changes in the thug's eyes. It might be recognition. It might be confusion. He says, 'I don't know what you're talking about.' He tries to snarl the words, but his voice is unsteady.

Luke can't read the man's face. Relief and fury alternate within him as he tries to find the answer. Recognition or confusion? Was it me or was it them? He knows he can't have done it. He can't have. And yet, if these kids didn't do it, who did?

As Luke's body moves into the other man's, he sees the black dog's knotted muscles move under her satin fur. Hard and soft. Hard and soft. As Luke throws the man back onto the tray—again, that dull thud of a skull hitting metal—he sees the white glint of the black dog's canines. White against black. White against black. As Luke clasps the man's struggling wrists in one of his massive hands, he remembers the dog snapping and growling when he'd first tried to scare her off. She was never aggressive, Luke realises, gazing at the man pinned under him. She was just scared, scared for her life.

Carefully, Luke clamps his free hand across the man's throat. Feels rough stubble. The buoyant hardness of his

Adam's apple. Presses his palm down onto the warm, damp skin. The man spits and gurgles. Luke lets him. Lets him taste suffocation. Lets him fall towards unconsciousness. Luke lifts his hand. Waits for him to get his breath back—to return fully to his ordeal. Luke watches his ruined thumb hover over a pale, darting eye. Sees the shut and crusted eye of the black dog. Presses downwards. The man begins to chant, 'No, no, no.' The girl begins to whisper, 'God, Oh God, Oh God.' Luke feels excitement power through him. She's right, he thinks, she's right. I can blind this man. I can press his eye into the thicks of his skull. I can kill him. I can thump her and fuck her and then fuck her again. The man begins to whisper, 'I'm sorry, I'm sorry.' Luke watches. Listens. He cannot tell if the man beneath him is making a confession or begging for his life. Quietly, Luke asks, 'Sorry for what?' He keeps the pressure of his thumb even and balanced. The man's eye is his new centre of gravity. 'For everything,' the man gasps. 'Everything. *Everything.*' Suddenly the man stops begging and bracing. Stops struggling. Nothing moves except for his tears.

Luke thinks of Miriam, crying eternally over her till in the office. Thinks of little Charlie, with all her bruises and bravado, crying over her cooking. Thinks of Quang, crying over his ruined feet. Thinks, with a blister of pain, of the black dog crying into the mud, crying into his chest, crying herself to death. Luke stares down at the thug's face and presses harder. He looks down and sees Miriam's Jamie—her son, her nephew—paralysed with shyness. Sees Dave choking on his loves and his hates. Sees Cane destroying everything around him, unstoppable. Luke presses harder. Sees himself hunting with his dad and his mates around the farm. Sees how they cared for the animals they bred to kill, and killed the animals that preyed to live. Feels the scalps of the foxes and feral dogs, wet and warm in his hand. Presses harder. Sees his dad's downcast eyes on that final scorching morning, when Luke saluted him and then left for the city. Left him to kill himself, by himself. Goddamn you, Luke thinks. Goddamn you, Dad, you coward.

Luke presses the hot, hard eye. Harder, harder. Sees the terrified face of the chef who'd watched as—in a split second, with merely the flick of his wrist—the oil in his pan fried off Luke's skin. For the first time Luke understands what the expression on that face was. Not spite. Not anger. Not pleasure. But horror. Disbelief. It was a face swamped by an instant and complete grief. Luke presses down, harder. Sees all of the people who couldn't face him afterwards. Sees Sarah, the one person who dared look at him. Sees her seeing him, just as the brindle dog and the black dog looked at him and saw him and demanded he look back. Luke presses harder. Sees himself alone in his unit, walking circles between the TV and the computer, doing nothing except all the pointless poisonous things he can't stop himself doing. Presses harder. Looks down. In the thug's one exposed eye he recognises the glassy stare of the brindle dog. Senses the same silent question travelling the air between them. What did I do? What did I do wrong?

Luke stares. Sees that his thumb is about to blind another man's eye. Lifts his hand away. Stands and turns and walks through the petrified forest of the others. Looks at the kids in the dirt by the fire. Sees that they are crying like babies. Sees that they *are* babies. Walks on. Disappears into the quarry's shadows. Leaves all of them, all of it, behind. Walks up the path. Again, he expects the dog to appear by his side. Again, he falls into that agonising gap between habit and remembrance. And again, the heart-stab of those unanswered questions. Who did it? Was it me? Of course not. (But I've done it before. I've done it before.) Was it them? And does it matter? *Does it matter?*

Luke walks along the edge of the lake. Looks out at the rock wall dividing the glittering dark. Remembers the soft warmth and breathing silence of the dog sitting next to him out there. Keeps walking. Tries to stop his stupid body calling out for her, begging her to come back, begging her to forgive him—if it was him. On he walks. Sees Cane and Miriam, gripped and driven by things they could not—cannot—control. Luke tries to shake off the feeling he had in the office with them. He can't bear it. The idea that there's no pattern to any of it. No meaning. No sense. That none of them are anything more than specks of sand in a dust storm. What does it matter! (Does it matter? Does it matter?) This chaos burned off my skin, created Cane and all the other bastards like him. But it also created the lake, brought me the black dog, and gave me Miriam. Luke remembers those first seconds when she was in his arms. Still, the idea of it seems as unlikely and ugly as any of his imaginings with Sarah. But I didn't imagine it. And it wasn't ugly. It was its own thing. It is our own thing. It is her body and mine, meeting in their own way. It is her body telling mine: It's not what you think that matters, it's what you do. *Hold me.*

He walks past his old bench. Wanders up the overgrown, looping track to the gate. Anger and fear shiver through him. Of course it matters who tortured the black dog. But he'll never know. And no matter what he did to her—no matter what he's done in the past— tonight, he didn't do it.

I didn't do what I could have done.

Didn't do what every cell in my body wanted me to do.

Didn't do what I once would have relished as my right.

I didn't do it. I didn't do it.

And I'll never do it again. Because that's not me. Not anymore.

Ø

Luke sits on the bench, collar up, arms crossed against the bluster, and looks out across the grey. He's watching her struggle with her board and her huge red kite. He sees her yanked under the chopped surface. Sees her thrashing and sinking. Sees her wetsuit becoming heavier, slicker, blacker, bloated. Sees her motionless, and then rising up again, halting, floating like a human balloon in the toxic grey silence, the ropes and pulleys of her harness tangled forever in the forests of trash below. Right where she belongs.

Later, when he walks up to the gate along the overgrown gravel path, he sees her again. Sees her muscles move under the smooth skin of her long legs. Counts the knobbles of her spine through her thin top. Doesn't cough to warn her of his approach. Not this time. Instead, he comes up suddenly, right next to her. She jerks to a stop. Gasps. Her face flushes with recognition and fear. He stares into her pale sandy-lashed eyes. Stares into her until she—not he, this time, *not he*—looks away. 'It's not safe,' he'd said, months ago, trying to warn her of the lake's dangers. Today, he says nothing.

He watches the girl shrink. He does not feel the same sick twist of pleasure and pain he felt the first time they met. He just wonders if she shrinks out of fear or shame. If they were the ones who did it, was she there? And if she was, did she try to stop them? Or did she get off on it too?

Luke lets her cower. He sees her grabbing at her guy, fucking and being fucked while the other boys and men wander off in anger and embarrassment and envy. Sees her sitting on the end of the ute. A princess. A queen. Her arms and legs locked with her man's. Her prince. Their bastard king. He looks down at the stars tattooed across her feet. No, he thinks. You're no sky walker. You can't fly. They're not stars, just scars, written in ink, flecked with dirt.

He walks on. Leaves her alone on the track. They were never my thoughts, he thinks. They were never my words.

When he reaches the gate he pauses. For the hundredth time habit makes him turn and look back to see if the dog is there, watching him go. The black dog. Not his dog. Not the lake's. Not the quarry's. Nobody's dog. Her own dog. Always and forever her own dog, hunting him through the dark, stalking him into friendship.

ACKNOWLEDGMENTS

I'D LIKE TO thank the Australia Council for the financial support they gave me to create this short story collection.

Thanks also to the literary journals who have supported my work through publication: 'Quarry', *Griffith Review*, No. 50, November, 2015; 'Morning Song', *Griffith Review*, No. 40, April, 2013; 'The Ferryman', *Overland*, No. 211, Winter, 2013; 'Eat. Shit. Die.', *Meanjin*, Vol. 71, No. 4, Summer, 2012; 'Gently, Gently', *Antipodes*, Vol. 25, No. 2, December, 2011; 'The Broken Body', *Meanjin*, Vol. 70, No. 3, Spring, 2011; 'Adrian', *Southerly*, Vol. 69, No. 1, 2009; 'The Wished For', *Westerly*, Vol. 51, November, 2006; 'What There Is', *Voiceworks*, Winter, Issue 57, 2004.

I'd like to acknowledge the years of mentorship and friendship I've received from the writers Andrea Goldsmith and Philip Salom.

Especial thanks to Caroline and John Wood, and the team at Margaret River Press, for giving me, and so many Australian writers, the opportunity to give our stories a 'paper home' in a world where more and more words disappear into the ether. Thanks also to Susan Miller who designed the book and its wonderful cover.

Finally, I'd like to thank Josephine Taylor who edited this collection. Your wisdom, thoroughness, encouragement and patience has helped me develop these stories to their full potential. You have shown me how the editing and writing processes can unite in a true collaboration.